The Whispers

Also by Greg Howard

Middle School's a Drag, You Better Werk!

Social Intercourse

The Whispers

GREG HOWARD

PUFFIN BOOKS

PUFFIN BOOKS
An imprint of Penguin Random House LLC, New York

First published in the United States of America by G. P. Putnam's Sons, 2019
Published by Puffin Books, an imprint of Penguin Random House LLC, 2020

Visit us online at penguinrandomhouse.com

THE LIBRARY OF CONGRESS HAS CATALOGED THE G. P. PUTNAM'S SONS EDITION AS FOLLOWS:
Names: Howard, Greg (Gregory Steven), author.
Title: The Whispers / Greg Howard.
Description: New York, NY: G. P. Putnam's Sons Books for Young Readers, 2019.
Summary: "Eleven-year-old Riley's mom has disappeared and Riley knows that if
he leaves tributes for the Whispers, magical fairies that grant wishes, his mom will
come back to him"—Provided by publisher.
Identifiers: LCCN 2018022153 | ISBN 9780525517498 (hardback)
| ISBN 9780525517504 (ebook)
Subjects: | CYAC: Family life—South Carolina—Fiction. | Missing persons—Fiction.
| Wishes—Fiction. | Magic—Fiction. | Gays—Fiction. | South Carolina—Fiction. |
Mystery and detective stories. | BISAC: JUVENILE FICTION / Fantasy & Magic.
Classification: LCC PZ7.1.H6877 Whi 2019 | DDC [Fic]—dc23
LC record available at https://lccn.loc.gov/2018022153

Puffin Books ISBN 9780525517511

Printed in the United States of America

Design by Dave Kopka
Text set in Janson MT Pro

7 9 10 8 6

For Mama and Daddy,

and for Tucker—the greatest dog in the history of dogs

Hope is being able to see that there is light despite all of the darkness.

—DESMOND TUTU

There once was a boy who heard the Whispers.

He heard them late in the day as the lazy sun dipped below the treetops and the woods behind his house came alive with the magic of twilight. The voices came to him so gently he thought it might be the wind, or the first trickle of summer rain. But as time passed, the voices grew louder and the boy was sure they were calling his name. So he followed them.

The Whispers led the boy to a clearing deep in the woods where a rotted old tree stump sat in the center and fallen leaves covered the ground like crunchy brown carpet. The boy stood next to the stump, waited, and listened. He couldn't see the Whispers, but he knew they were there. Their wispy voices surrounded him, tickling the rims of his ears and filling every darkened shadow of the forest.

After waiting patiently for quite some time, the Whispers' garbled words finally began to make sense to the boy, and they told him things. The Whispers knew everything—all the secrets of the universe. They told the boy what color the moon was up close and how many miles of ocean covered the Earth. They even told him how long he would live—26,332 days. The boy was pleased, because that sounded like a good long time to him. But as they continued to whisper knowledge into his ear, they never showed themselves to the boy. He only caught glimpses from the corner of his eye of their faint bluish glow fading in and out around him. He so badly wanted to see them, to know what kind of creatures they were. How big were they? Or how tiny? Were they thin, or fat, or hairy? Were they made of skin and bones like him, or of tree bark, or leaves, or dirt? Or something else entirely?

The Whispers told the boy that if he brought them tributes, they would give him his heart's desires. The boy wasn't sure what a tribute was and he didn't want very much anyway. He could hardly call them heart's desires. Maybe a new pair of sneakers so the kids at school wouldn't tease him about his raggedy old ones. Maybe a better job for his father so he wouldn't worry so much about money. And he would love to see his mother smile again, something she rarely did anymore. But he guessed what he really wanted was to see the Whispers with his very own eyes.

One day, as the boy's mother made a batch of her special blackberry jam, he asked her what a *tribute* was. She thought about it a moment and finally told him that a tribute was like a gift to show respect. The boy eyed his mother's handiwork spread over the kitchen table. Everyone loved her jam. When she took it to the local farmers market, she always sold out. And her blackberry jam was his personal favorite. He was sure it would make an excellent tribute for the Whispers. When his mother left the room, the boy took one of the jars from the table and hid it under his bed.

The following afternoon, as the sun was setting, he went back to the clearing in the woods with the jam tucked under his arm. He left it sitting on the rotted old tree stump for the Whispers. Satisfied with his tribute, the boy spoke his heart's desires aloud and then hurried home as not to scare the Whispers away.

When the boy's father got home from work that evening, his mood was lighter than usual and the lines of worry had completely vanished from his face. He told the family that he'd received a promotion at work and tomorrow the boy's mother should take him shopping to buy him new clothes and shoes for school. This news made his mother smile. The boy was amazed that he'd received three of his heart's desires with only one jar of jam. Surely the Whispers would reveal themselves to him if he took them a tribute even better than a jar of his mother's blackberry jam. And he knew just the thing.

The next day, when the boy returned from shopping with his mother, he snuck out of the house right before sunset and took his new sneakers to the clearing in the woods. He kept them in the box, neatly wrapped in tissue paper so they wouldn't get scuffed or dirty. They were the nicest shoes he'd ever owned, and surely this tribute would persuade the Whispers to show themselves.

When he approached the rotted old tree stump, he saw that the blackberry jam was gone. The boy wasn't surprised. He was sure the Whispers enjoyed his mother's jam just as much as everyone else did. He put the box with his sneakers on top of the rotted old tree stump, stood back, and waited. And waited. And waited. He waited so long, he wasn't sure the Whispers were pleased enough with his tribute.

Finally something tickled the back of his neck with the lightest flutter of breath grazing his skin. It spoke his name and asked him what he wished. The boy froze. The Whispers had never come that close before. They must be pleased with his tribute after all. He was excited, but afraid if he moved it would scare them away, so he closed his eyes and remained perfectly still.

"I wish to see you," the boy said in barely a whisper of his own. "I want to know what you look like. It's my heart's desire."

At first there was no clear answer, only a garble of Whispers conversation that he couldn't understand. Then the words slowly pieced themselves together like a puzzle in his ear.

"If we reveal ourselves, you can never leave us," the Whispers said, their velvety voices caressing his ear through the warm summer breeze. "You must stay here in the woods with us forever, for you will know everything, and that is a burden too great to bear in your world."

The boy swallowed hard. He closed his eyes even tighter and stood very still as sweat trailed down his neck, the Whispers' words chilling him from head to toe.

"Are you sure this is what you wish?" the Whispers asked. "To see us? To stay with us and become a whisper in the wind?"

The boy began to worry. He thought about all the things he would miss if he stayed in the woods with the Whispers forever. He would never get to ride his bike again, or go swimming in the pond with his friends. And he would never see his mother and father again. It seemed like an awfully high price to pay just to see what the Whispers looked like. Besides, he'd already offered them his brand-new sneakers, and they were the nicest things he owned. Wasn't that enough?

"No," the Whispers said, reading his thoughts. "It is not enough. If you see us, you must become one of us. And then you will know everything there is to know. You will hear everything. See everything. But the only tribute we can accept for that is your soul."

The boy stood there with his eyes closed tight, scared he might accidentally see one of the Whispers and then the choice would be made for him. He needed a moment to think. The boy wondered what else there was to know. Because of the Whispers he knew the color of the moon up close, how many miles of ocean covered the Earth, and how long he would live—26,332 days. He knew he had a home to which he could return. He knew his parents loved him and his father worked hard to take care of their family. And the kids at school would tease him a little less now that he had brand-new sneakers.

The boy knew it would be dark soon and if he waited too long he might never find his way out of the woods. Then what would the Whispers do with him? He felt around until he found the box with his sneakers on the tree stump. He grabbed it, turned, and ran as fast as he could. He held the box close to his chest and didn't dare open his eyes. He tripped and fell. Got back up and ran into one tree after another. Branches whacked him across the face and chest, but he kept running blindly through the woods.

Only after he'd gone a good long ways and the tiny voices had faded behind him did the boy dare open his eyes. Even then he was careful not to look around. He stared straight ahead until he got to the tree line and ran the whole way home, never looking back, not even when he reached his house.

After that the boy never heard the Whispers again, but he didn't mind. He already had his heart's desires. He had his mother. And his father. And his friends. And his brand-new sneakers. Plus he knew what color the moon was up close, how many miles of ocean covered the Earth, and how long he would live—26,332 days. He didn't know *all* the secrets of the universe and maybe he never would, but he knew plenty.

This was Mama's favorite story. She told me the story every night until the day she disappeared. Then I started hearing the Whispers.
And I followed them.

1

THE WORLD'S WORST POLICE DETECTIVE

Fat Bald Detective thinks I had something to do with it. He doesn't come right out and say it, but the way he repeats the same questions over and over—like if he keeps on asking them, I might crack under the pressure—well, it's pretty clear that I'm suspect number one. I don't know why he thinks I'm guilty, other than the fact that he's not very smart. He's not nearly as good at this as the cops on TV, and they're only actors. He just sits there smiling at me, waiting for me to say something more. But I don't know what he wants from me. I mean, sure I have secrets. Big ones. The kind of secrets you take to your grave. But I would never hurt anyone on purpose. Especially not Mama.

I push my hair out of my eyes and look up at the clock on the wall. It shouldn't be too much longer. Maybe I can just wait him out. I look at the desk in the corner of the cramped office. It's cluttered with books, stacks of file folders, and a darkened computer screen decorated with a rainbow of Post-it notes because Fat Bald Detective can't remember anything. There isn't one inch of clear space anywhere to be seen on his desk. It's very unprofessional.

That was one of our words from the calendar—I think from last January. It's still on my wall.

Unprofessional is when someone or something doesn't look or act right in the workplace.

Good, Button. Now use it in a sentence, Mama would say if she were here.

Then I would say something like, *Fat Bald Detective's office is very unprofessional because there's crap everywhere and it smells like Fritos.*

That would have made Mama laugh. I could always make her laugh when we played the word-of-the-day game. Mama says it's okay if you don't always remember the exact dictionary definition of a word as long as you can describe the meaning in your own words and you can use it in a sentence. Now that I think of it, there should be a picture of Fat Bald Detective's office beside the word *unprofessional* in the dictionary.

His office is nothing like the ones in the police stations on TV. There aren't any bright fluorescent lights in here, or cool floor-to-ceiling walls of glass so he can see the whole department and wave someone in at a moment's notice just to yell at them. There's only one small window with a view of the parking lot, and Fat Bald Detective seems to prefer table lamps to fluorescent lighting. And although you can't smell the offices of the police stations on TV, I always imagined they'd smell like leftover pizza and cigarette smoke—not Fritos. I guess it's better than doing this in one of their interrogation rooms. At least in here there's a couch for me to sit on before they lock me up and throw away the keys. Then it hits me. It's the couch. The couch smells like Fritos.

"And what happened after that, Riley?" Fat Bald Detective says—*again*.

Fat Bald Detective has a name. It's Frank. He said I could call him Frank the first time he brought me in for questioning. Mama doesn't normally approve of us calling adults by their first name, but Frank told me to and he's the law. I figure I should probably cooperate as much as possible so he doesn't get any more suspicious than he already is.

Frank actually has three names. They're all printed on his door and on the triangle nameplate on his desk. Grandma says that people who use three names are *puttin' on airs*, but I don't think Frank has any airs to put on. He's short, and bald, and round, and looks like Mr. Potato Head without the tiny black hat, so I think *Fat Bald Detective* every time I look at him.

"I don't remember," I say.

He keeps asking me what happened that day and I keep telling him I don't remember. We've played this little game for almost four months now. I was ten when we started. I'm a whole different age now. I've had a birthday and a summer break since then. I even moved up a grade in school. Detective Chase Cooper on *Criminal Investigative*

Division: Chicago can solve a case in an hour. Forty-four minutes if you fast-forward through the commercials. But Frank will never be as smart as Detective Chase Cooper. Or as handsome. Frank's really not a bad guy, though. He means well. But I don't think he's ever going to crack this case, at least not before I turn twelve. He's running out of time. So is Mama.

Frank and his officers should be out there trying to find the perp—following up on leads, canvassing the neighborhood. That's the way they do it on TV, and they *always* catch the guy. They don't sit in poorly lit rooms that smell like Fritos questioning the eleven-year-old son of the missing person over and over. But maybe this is just the way cops do things out here in the country. Maybe they don't watch much TV.

"Tell me again what you do remember," Frank says in that smiley-calm voice of his that I hate. Like I'm ten or something and if he talks real soft and slow, I'll spill my guts.

I sigh as loudly as I can, just so my irritation is clear. "Like I already said, Mama was taking a nap on the sofa in the living room."

It *was* strange because we only use the living room for special occasions, like on Christmas morning to open presents, or when the preacher from North Creek Church of God used to visit. Somehow the couch in the living room is called a *sofa* and the one in the den is just a *couch*. The living room furniture is not very comfortable, but Mama says it's not supposed to be. Like that makes any sense—furniture that's meant to be uncomfortable. I've told Frank all that before, so I don't repeat it. I've learned only to repeat the important stuff. Otherwise Frank finds new questions to ask. I don't like new questions.

Frank laces his fingers together on top of his basketball of a belly and smiles again. I don't like his smile. It looks like a plastic piece of Mr. Potato Head's face that he can pop on and off anytime he wants.

"And where were you while your mother was lying down in the living room?"

I roll my eyes at him. Daddy wouldn't like that.

Be respectful of authority, he would say. *Frank is just trying to help.*

But I've answered this same question so many times. If he can't remember, then why doesn't he write it down on one of his five thousand rainbow Post-it notes, or turn on a tape recorder like they do on TV. I wonder where he went to detective school. Probably one of those online courses, but poor Frank got ripped off. If Mama were here, she'd add a *bless his heart.* It sounds nice, but I don't think it's meant to be.

"I was outside playing with my friends," I say.

Frank raises a bushy eyebrow at me. "And . . ."

"And when I came back inside, Mama was lying on the sofa in the living room. Like I just said."

"And then what did you do?" the world's worst police detective asks.

"I touched her hand to see if she was asleep." I say it like I'm quoting a Bible verse I've been forced to memorize and recite on command.

Frank looks down his snap-on nose at me. "And how did it feel, touching her hand?"

This is a new one. What the heck does he mean, how did it feel? It felt like skin and Jergens hand lotion, that's how. And how is this going to help them find Mama? Why doesn't Frank ask me more about the suspicious car that was parked in front of the house that day? I told him about it the first time they hauled me down here for questioning, but he hasn't asked about it since. Instead he's wasting time asking about me touching Mama's hand. *World's. Worst. Police. Detective. Ever.*

"She felt a little chilled, so I pulled the cover up over her hands. I didn't want to wake her, so I went back outside to play."

Frank scrunches his face like that wasn't the answer he was looking for. He thinks I'm hiding something. Like *I'm* a suspect, which is crazy because I want them to find her. I promise I do.

"And that's the last thing you remember?" he says. "Touching your mother's hand while she was lying down on the sofa? Nothing else?"

He knows it is. Unless he somehow found out about Kenny from Kentucky. Or the ring.

Stick to your story, I tell myself. That's what people on TV who are accused of a crime always say—*stick to your story and everything will be fine.* No one has actually accused me of anything yet. But they might as well, the way they all look at me—like they know I'm hiding something.

"Yes, sir," I say, being respectful of authority. Even Frank's authority. "That's the last thing I remember."

Frank squints his eyes at me. Yep. He thinks I'm lying. Or crazy. Or both. But technically I'm not lying. Kenny from Kentucky is long gone and they've never asked me about the ring, so I've never told them. Besides, Daddy will blister my hide if he finds out I have it. I wonder if the ring is considered evidence. Can they put me in jail for withholding evidence? I think there was an episode of *CID: Chicago* about that. I can't remember what happened, but I'm sure Detective Chase Cooper solved the case in forty-four minutes.

Frank's talking now, but I can't understand what he's saying. His voice sounds like that teacher from *The Peanuts Movie*, which Mama and I watched together.

. . . wah waah wah wah, waah wah waah . . .

I nod my head every now and then to be polite and respectful. Frank has some real wacky theories about what might have happened to Mama that day, so whenever he starts speculating like this, I turn on my internal Charlie Brown teacher translator.

Speculating is like when poorly educated police detectives make dumb guesses about a case without having any evidence.

Use it in a sentence, Button, I imagine Mama saying.

Frank needs to get off his big round behind, stop speculating about what happened that day, and go find Mama before it's too late.

Frank glances over at the clock and lets out one of his *this isn't getting us anywhere* sighs because he knows I'm not listening anymore.

"Your father's probably waiting for you outside," he says. "You know, Riley, it's been nearly four months now. I'd much rather you tell me what happened on your own, but if you can't—or won't—I can help you fill in some of the blanks if you'll let me."

Oh crap. I know what Frank's talking about from the cop shows on TV. It's when they start telling the perp what *they* think happened. They make their accusations over and over, louder and louder, until the perp finally confesses.

"How's the case going?" I ask, changing the subject. "Any new leads? New information? Have you found their car yet?"

Frank inhales slowly, then releases a long stream of sour-smelling air through puckered lips. "There's no new information, Riley. You know that." He stands and waves me toward the door. "If you remember anything before I see you again, have your dad call me, okay? It's very important."

I get up and walk out, shaking my head so Frank knows what a disappointment he is to me. What are we paying these people for with Daddy's hard-earned tax dollars if they can't even find my mama?

2

TWENTY-EIGHT WORDS
IN THREE DAYS

We eat supper early that night—just the three of us at the kitchen table. We haven't eaten in the dining room since Mama disappeared. We used to eat dinner in there every night. Now it sits dark and empty like a tomb or a shrine. I don't think we'll use it again until Mama comes home safe and we can all sit in there as a family again. We can eat, and talk, and laugh like we used to. Daddy will tell lame jokes, Mama will ask us about our day at school, and my brother won't be mean to me anymore. But for now it's just a dark room collecting dust on our memories of her.

We sit in silence, Danny wolfing down his mashed potatoes like it's his last meal ever, and Daddy staring at his plate like he's reading tea leaves. Every couple of minutes, he moves some food around with his fork, but that's about it. He hasn't always been like this, just since Mama was taken. I don't think he knows how to *be*, without her here holding us all together. That was her department, not his.

Before Mama disappeared, Daddy laughed a lot. And he always loved scaring Danny and me, or pinning us down on the floor and tickling us until we almost peed ourselves. He'd do the same thing to Mama sometimes until she would scream and laugh and holler like a crazy person. Now when I look over at Daddy, all I can see is the bald spot on top of his head. I don't think he likes to look at us anymore, least of all me. I know it's because I can't remember what happened that day. And because I look the most like her. And because Mama and I share a name and a birthday. But also because of *my condition*.

Or maybe he blames me and that's why he can't look at me. Maybe he thinks I could have done something to save her. Called out for help. Gotten the license plate number of the fancy car that was sitting in front of the house that day. Locked the front door after I went outside. But Mama was in the house, so why would I lock the door? And how did I know something bad was going to happen to her? She just disappeared without a trace, right out of our front living room. That's another reason we don't go in there anymore. It's like a crime scene that no one wants to disturb in case there's still some undiscovered shred of evidence hidden in there. Fibers in the carpet or something. I'm surprised Frank hasn't put bright yellow police tape across the door. Maybe he should. Who am I to say? Detective Chase Cooper would know what to do.

Since no one is talking or looking up, I glance around the kitchen as I pretend to eat. I see Mama in every nook and cranny. Like the dish towels hanging on the oven door handle with the words *As for me and my house, we will serve the*

Lord embroidered on them in red frilly letters. I was with her when she found those at the Big Lots in Upton. She loved them so much she bought two sets. But that's not a lot of money at the Big Lots. Probably like three dollars or something. And the Precious Moments cookie jar on the counter—she found that at the Salvation Army store. It has a picture on the front of a boy and a girl with really big heads and droopy eyes sitting back to back on a tree stump.

Love one another.

Mama likes things with nice sayings printed on them.

She says, *It can't hurt to be reminded to love each other every time you reach for a cookie, right, Button?*

Mama loves baking cookies. She makes them for me to take to school for my teachers and to sell at Mr. Killen's Market to raise money for the church. She even made a big batch last Christmas for the prisoners at the work camp outside of Upton. She's real good at cookies, but one time she tried making me blackberry jam like in the story of the Whispers and it was terrible. It was so bad that we laughed and laughed while we ate some of it on toast that I burnt. Another time she tried to teach me how to make biscuits and gravy, but I burned my hand on the stove, so that was the end of my cooking lessons.

All I'm allowed to make now are frozen fish sticks and Tater Tots in the oven. Frozen fish sticks are gross but we've eaten them a lot the last four months. I don't mind the Tater Tots. But Grandma supplied tonight's meal even though Daddy tells her she doesn't have to do that anymore.

Grandma hates the idea of us eating fish sticks and Tater Tots so much. I wonder what Mama's eating right now. Or if she's been eating at all. What if whoever took her doesn't give her enough food to stay alive until the police can find her?

"Frank said there aren't any new leads in the case," I say, breaking the unbearable silence. My words hang in the air like lint.

Daddy looks up from his plate and stares like he doesn't even recognize me. Danny stops eating and glares at me from across the table. He never wants to talk about Mama's case. Even Tucker lets out an anxious groan under the table, like he knows I should have kept my big mouth shut. He misses Mama too. He hasn't been the same since she disappeared, but the vet can't figure out what's wrong with him. I think he's just depressed.

"Finish your peas and take Tucker outside," Daddy says, looking back down at his plate.

I think that makes a total of two dozen words Daddy's said to me in three days, so I hit the jackpot this evening. I eat my peas one at a time and with my fingers. I know it annoys him. If Mama were here, she'd give me the Mama side-eye. But she's not. And Daddy doesn't even look up to scold me. He just plows circles in his mashed potatoes with his fork. If Danny or I did that, he would yell at us and tell us to stop playing with our food.

Daddy used to like me. He even took me on my very first roller coaster ride, and he wanted it to be the same one he took his first ride on—the Swamp Fox at Family Kingdom Amusement Park in Myrtle Beach. It's one of those old-timey wooden coasters that make that loud *clack, clack, clack* noise when they go up the first climb. The newer coasters don't make that sound anymore and Daddy says it's not the same without it. I was so scared and screamed my butt off the entire ride, but Daddy didn't mind. He just laughed and laughed like a crazy person with his hands raised high in the air the whole time.

When I was six, we were on vacation in Florida and Daddy took us to an alligator farm. He picked me up so I could get a better look at the big, slimy creatures. Then he thought it would be real funny to pretend like he was going to throw me over the fence like gator bait. A fat one spotted us and slowly came crawling our way while Daddy kept up his act for *way* too long, swinging me back and forth and back and forth.

One, two . . .

On *three*, I almost crapped my pants. But he never got to three, so I'm pretty sure Daddy wasn't trying to feed me to the alligators. I screamed bloody murder anyway. But Daddy didn't mind. He just laughed and laughed like a crazy person. To this day I can't even look at an alligator on TV. But I have to admit, it was fun. Daddy was fun. Not anymore.

Danny's phone vibrates on the table, which gets him a hard look from Daddy. His phone is supposed to be off during dinner. Danny grabs it and tucks it into his lap. It's probably some girl from school calling. Danny likes girls now. *Ugh.*

"Sorry," he says to Daddy without looking him in the eye.

Daddy stares at him a moment, and finally his face softens. Just a tad. He doesn't yell at Danny. He would have yelled at me, but Danny's a daddy's boy just as much as I'm a mama's boy. And I don't have a phone yet. It's okay. I wouldn't want any girls calling me anyway.

Daddy gets up and goes to the window over the sink. He mumbles as he lifts it open, "It's stifling in here."

Wow. Twenty-eight words in three days. But those last four I have to share with Danny.

"What does that mean, Daddy?" I say, although I have a pretty good idea. I just want him to notice me.

"What does what mean?" he kind of grunts back.

"*Stifling.*"

He looks over his shoulder at me and gives me a flat look. "It means it's hot and stuffy."

I push my luck, trying to lighten the mood. "Use it in a sentence, Daddy."

He squints at me like he can't remember my name or why I'm here. "What?"

"Use the word *stifling* in a sentence," I say, feeling hopeful.

"I just did." He looks out the window, dismissing me with a slight shake of his head.

Danny stuffs his mouth and grunts his agreement with Daddy. Danny eats like a pig and always sides with Daddy.

Actually Danny does *everything* Daddy does, so now that Daddy doesn't like me, Danny doesn't either. He used to play with me before Mama disappeared. Now he just acts like I don't exist. He barely even talks to me. Stays in his room with the door closed doing Lord knows what, and hangs out with his new high school friends in Upton. He's only three years older than me, but he treats me like a baby.

Tucker must have sensed the tension in the room, because he lets out a long, flappy fart that sounds like a balloon deflating under the table. Danny looks at me and his lips curl up, exposing teeth caked with mashed potatoes and gravy. Danny never smiles at me anymore, but he thinks farts are hilarious. Especially dog farts. Even I can't help but smirk, just a little. But we both freeze, waiting to see how Daddy will respond. It could go either way. The seconds tick by long and slow like they did during the sermons at North Creek Church of God when we used to be churchgoing people.

I dare to look over at Daddy standing at the sink. His shoulders are shaking a little. Laughing or crying, I can't tell. He turns to face us and I see that it's both. He's laughing softly, but at the same time his eyes are moist. I'm surprised because I don't think I've seen Daddy crack even a polite smile to anyone in the last four months. His laughter sparks life into the room and we know it's okay now. We have permission to join him, and we do. Hard. It's the first time since Mama disappeared that there's been any laughter in this house. It sounds amazing, echoing around the kitchen and then drifting out the window. Tucker scrambles from under the table, barking excitedly and joining in our rare moment of happiness. Daddy's laughter eventually dies down, though. His smile doesn't totally disappear, but it fades a little. His eyes are still misty.

A strong honeysuckle-scented breeze rolls in through the open window and brushes my cheeks. I close my eyes and breathe it in deep. It's almost like she's here, like she heard us laughing and rushed into the kitchen to see what all the fuss was about. Mama loves the smell of honeysuckle. She always yells at Daddy for cutting back the bushes in the yard. It grows like crazy around our house. Mama taught me how to pinch off the bottom of the blooms, slide the stem out, and lick the nectar off. She calls it nature's candy. Now whenever I catch a whiff of honeysuckle, I think of her and I wonder if I'll ever see her again. Right now, it's like she's reaching out to me from wherever she's being held captive—calling to me to come find her. To rescue her. The police are useless, so I may be her only hope.

"Take that gassy mutt outside, Riley," Daddy says, his smile completely fading.

Wow. He said my name. And he wasn't yelling or cross sounding or anything. Just said it like normal. Like he would say Danny's name. I hop out of my chair with a small jolt of satisfaction, or pride, or something pumping in my veins and guide Tucker to the kitchen door.

Looking back over my shoulder, I smile at him. "Okay, Daddy."

But he doesn't see me. He's already turned his back on us again. He stands at the sink, his shoulders shaking. I'm not sure if he's laughing again or if he's gone back to crying. I don't think I really want to know for sure, so I grab Tucker by the collar and hurry out the door.

3

PENTECOSTAL CORN CHOIR

Tucker shuffles down the steps ahead of me and goes directly to his favorite tree near the back of the yard. When he's finished marking his spot for like the thousandth time, he trots over to the edge of the Mathews family's cornfield, circles exactly three times, and squats to do his business. We don't charge Mr. Mathews for the extra fertilizer to that spot.

As I step down onto the grass, the warm glow of the setting sun blankets my face and a bully of a breeze comes out of nowhere and shoves me back. I hold up my hand, letting the honeysuckle-scented wind weave through my fingers like I do with Mama sometimes. But tonight it's like I'm trying to feel what direction she's in, as if the wind could tell me. It's that dimly lit sliver of the day when anything is possible. So why not look for magic? Why not hope? That's what Mama always says.

Walking over to the edge of the yard where Tucker is finishing up, I peer into the cornfield. Rows and rows of tall limber stalks sway back and forth in the wind, like a gospel choir of Pentecostal corn waving their green leafy hands in the air, praising Jesus. I can't stop myself from joining in and waving back at them, like I'm directing the Pentecostal corn choir, the way Mama and I used to do together almost every day at twilight.

"We need more from the altos, Mama," I say to her.

"They're giving you all they got, Button," she says, standing beside me, directing with one hand, the other resting on her hip. *"Barbara Jean has a cold."* She points to a wilting stalk of corn in the front row of the choir and we giggle. *"What about those tenors and basses?"*

Mama directs the sopranos and altos, and I'm in charge of the tenors and basses.

I make great big U-shaped motions with my arms, and nod down the row to a stalk the wind has knocked on its butt. "Brother Thompson was slain in the spirit, so we lost our best bass. And a couple of the tenors are busy speaking in tongues."

Mama looks over at me. Her eyes get real big and her lips curl up even though I can tell she's trying to fight it.

"Button!" She scolds with her eyes but she's losing it with her mouth. "That's borderline sacrilegious!"

I swing my arms back and forth. "Is that bad? I can't tell because you're grinning."

That makes Mama lose control of her face and laugh out loud.

"What does sacrilegious *mean, anyway?"* I say.

She scrunches up her face a second and then looks over at me. "It's when you poke fun of church stuff out loud, even though it really is secretly funny."

I grin back at her, directing away. "Use it in a sentence, Mama."

She points to the corn sopranos like they have a solo, encouraging them to sing out. "Button is a sinner who must repent this Sunday at church for being sacrilegious about speaking in tongues and being slain in the spirit."

This makes us both laugh hard. Mama's a real soloist in the North Creek Church of God human person choir. And singing was her talent in all three of the beauty pageants she won—Miss Myrtle Beach (sponsored by Dollar General), Miss Buckingham County (sponsored by Mr. Killen's Market), and Mrs. Upton (sponsored by Daniel James—Independent Contractor and Daddy). I love to hear Mama sing. Everybody does. She's especially good on the old hymns of the church.

We turn our attention back to the corn choir, and Mama feeds them the words.

Sowing in the morning, sowing seeds of kindness,
Sowing in the noontide and the dewy eve;
Waiting for the harvest, and the time of reaping,
We shall come rejoicing, bringing in the sheaves.

I bring the tenors and basses in and join her on the chorus, shout-singing at the top of my lungs to make her laugh.

A door slams somewhere behind me, and the memory gets swept up and carried away by the honeysuckle wind. Tucker barks once and runs off to the right. I look over my shoulder. Grandpa waves at me from the back porch of their house, which sits right next door to ours. I turn and aim my raised conducting arms at Grandpa, like I'm waving at him and wasn't just standing there directing the Pentecostal corn choir. They already think I'm crazy enough around here. No reason to give them more ammo. Something buzzes my ear with a wispy flutter that kind of tickles. I shake my head and slap it away. Probably just a moth. Moths creep me out.

Crossing our backyard, I head over to Grandpa, who gets no farther than the bottom of the porch steps before Tucker attacks him with sloppy kisses and nudges of his huge muzzle.

"That's my good boy," Grandpa says, leaning down and kissing Tucker on the top of his football-sized head.

He doesn't have to lean down too far. Part German shepherd and part Rottweiler, Tucker stands almost as tall as me. Daddy says if he'd known the tiny rescued pup he got me the day I was born would grow to one hundred and twenty pounds, he would have gotten me a cat like he did when Danny was born. The cat wandered off before Danny turned one. I guess she didn't like my brother very much, not even when he was a baby and rumored to be an abnormally beautiful child.

But Tucker's different from Danny's cat. When I'm home, he never leaves my side. The only person Tucker might love more than me is Mama, but he would never want me to know that. He wouldn't want to hurt my feelings.

When I reach them, Grandpa gives me an identical kiss on the top of my head, like Tucker and I are equals, but that's silly. No human person is as great as Tucker. The wind whips Grandpa's thick salt-and-pepper hair from side to side like a flag planted on top of his shoulders.

He stands up straight, shoves his hands in the pockets of his faded denim overalls, and cocks his head at me. "What're you doing out there staring at the corn, darlin'?"

Grandpa calls me *darlin'* sometimes. I don't know why, but it doesn't bother me the way it might bother other boys. It sounds natural coming from him. Actually it makes me feel special, because he never calls Danny *darlin'*. He calls Danny *sport*. I'm definitely not a *sport*.

I want to tell him that I'm worried about Mama. That I saw Detective Frank today and I don't think the investigation is going very well. But we're not supposed to talk about it. Nobody said so, but you can just tell. Daddy, Grandma, and Grandpa never bring up what happened to Mama. At least not when I'm around.

I look back at him and shake my head. "Nothing."

He eyes me like he might not believe me. I'm not as good a liar as Danny. But I don't want to make Grandpa sad. Mama is his and Grandma's only child since Uncle Mike died in Iraq exactly one month before I was born. They really love her a lot and she always made them so proud—straight-A student, church soloist, Sunday school teacher, all her charity work with prisoners and the poor, and a three-time beauty queen. She could have even been Miss South Carolina if she and Daddy hadn't eloped when she was nineteen. And Mama was their first and only child to graduate from college. She got her degree in social work. When I was a little kid, I used to think she got that degree to help her in her beauty pageants, but it turns out it's not that kind of social work at all.

I know her disappearance has been really hard on them. Grandpa can't even talk about her, and he made Grandma pack away all the pictures of Mama in their house. He said it was just too painful to see her face every day. I used to think it was just temporary and that they'll put the pictures back up when Mama comes home. But I'm beginning to wonder if they've given up hope of finding her like Daddy and Danny have. At least Grandpa doesn't drink anymore. He quit the Wild Turkey *cold* turkey the day Mama went missing and hasn't had a drop since. Grandma says she's thankful for small miracles 'cause she's been trying to get him to quit for years. Mama told me once that Grandpa started drinking when Uncle Mike died and sometimes it got real bad back then when I was just a baby. He never acted drunk around baby me, not that I can remember, so who am I to judge?

Grandpa clears his throat. "Your grandma is frying up some fatback. Come inside and have some with me."

"I already ate supper," I say.

Grandpa gives me the ear. That's when he can't hear

you, so he cups his hand around the rim of his ear and leans forward.

I point over to our house and raise my voice to Grandpa levels. "Already ate."

He nods. Less words, more volume usually does the trick with him.

He puts his arm around my shoulders and guides me. "Well then, just come in and say hello to Grandma. You know she loves to see you. She's making fruit salad too."

Grandma's fruit salad is no joke, so I don't resist. Tucker leads us, making himself right at home, going up the stairs of their back porch and pawing at the door until Grandpa opens it for him. Tucker thinks he's one of the grandkids. And let's face it, he is.

Before I go inside, I turn one last time and stare out at the cornfield. Something about the wind tonight—the way it sounds like the ocean in my ears, and the honeysuckle-scented sky, and the Pentecostal corn choir waving their arms at me. It's like the whole world is trying to tell me something. Maybe it's trying to help me remember the song Mama used to sing to me every night after she told me the story of the Whispers, but I still can't remember it, as much as I try. It's stuck somewhere in the cloudy part of my brain.

I close my eyes, and mouth the wish that's become my nightly prayer. That the Whispers will speak to me. That they will help me find her. They know all the secrets of the universe, so they must know where Mama is. I wonder if it's sacrilegious to pray to the Whispers instead of God.

I know a lot of people have been praying to God about Mama and I guess He's been real busy or on vacation or something, because it sure hasn't helped. I don't think He's listening anymore, so I don't see any harm in praying to the Whispers. Maybe they're listening.

Mama says she hears them sometimes, but I never have. I've always wanted to hear them ever since Mama first started telling me the story. I would go stand out in the backyard at sunset and stare at the tree line beyond the cornfield, waiting for them. Wishing for them to talk to me like they talked to the boy in the story. They never did, so I gave up a long time ago. But since Mama went missing, I've started doing it again, every night for nearly four months, when I take Tucker out after supper at twilight. I haven't heard them, though. Not yet. But I'll keep wishing. And waiting. And listening. The Whispers are my only hope of finding her. I'm sure of it.

Another wall of honeysuckle-scented wind presses into my face. I lean into it and whisper into the dusky, half-lit world, just to remind them.

"I'm listening."

4

5-4-3-2-1 FRUIT SALAD

I sit at the kitchen table peeling apples with Grandpa's antique Swiss Army knife. He lets me play with it whenever I come over, but I'm not allowed to take it out of their house. Grandma would much rather I use a peeling knife, but this one fits in my hand perfectly and I feel like I'm representing the entire Swiss Army when I use it. I don't know how those Swiss soldiers defend themselves with such tiny weapons, but they're awfully handy. The handle is made of real wood, not plastic like the new ones. The wood's been rubbed smooth by decades of use by Grandpa and his daddy before him.

Great-Grandpa gave him the knife before Grandpa left for *the war*. That's about as much as Grandpa ever talks about *the war*. I don't know which war, because apparently there were several. I just hope Grandpa gives me the Swiss Army knife when I turn fourteen so I can use it when my best friend, Gary, and I go exploring in the woods. It makes sense that I would get it because when Danny turned fourteen, Grandpa gave him Uncle Mike's old twelve-gauge shotgun. Danny has been on a mission to rid the planet of squirrels ever since. I don't think there are any squirrels left in a five-mile radius of our house. But I don't want a gun. Guns scare me more than other boys. Mama doesn't like them either and was none too happy when Grandpa gave Danny the twelve-gauge.

"How many is that?" Grandma asks, her face drawn downward like it's been for months now.

"Two," I say.

I know it's only supposed to be two apples, but she always asks when I'm working on the last one to remind me. Mama calls that *passive-aggressive*. Grandma acts like three apples and not two would ruin the reputation of her fruit salad for all eternity. Grandma's 5-4-3-2-1 fruit salad is simple, but precise.

> *Five oranges*
> *Four bananas*
> *Three peaches*
> *Two apples*
> *And one package of Birds Eye Deluxe Halved Strawberries (in syrup)*

No frozen strawberry substitute will do. Grandma says it's what makes the whole thing taste right. Once Mr. Killen stopped carrying the Birds Eye frozen strawberries in his store and Grandma wrote him a letter of protest every week for two months until he brought them back. She almost started a petition.

That was one of our words from the calendar—April,

I think—but I already knew what it meant because of Grandma.

A *petition* is a paper that a ton of people sign when they get all riled up about something and want to get their way.

Like, *You don't mess with Grandma's 5-4-3-2-1 fruit salad unless you want a petition signed by everyone in Buckingham County who has ever tasted it.*

"BIRDS OF A FEATHER FLOCK TOGETHER!" Grandpa shouts from the other room.

He took his fatback into the den for *Wheel of Fortune*, a show he can watch without turning the volume up to high heaven. Every now and then he yells out a random phrase as he tries to solve the puzzles. He sounds crazy in there, but we pay him no mind, like Grandma says.

There's something I need to ask Grandma, but I don't know if it will make her cry. I hate it when Grandma cries and she's cried a lot in the last four months. She doesn't even try to hide it when she does. Just cries right out in front of God and everybody, like she's proud of it. She used to cry in church sometimes, but she hasn't set foot inside a church since Mama's disappearance. I think she's mad at God for taking both her children away from her and not answering her prayers to bring them home safe. I think that's fair.

I wipe the blade of the knife with a dish towel and look up at her. "Did you tell Mama the story of the Whispers when she was young?" I know she did. Mama told me so, but I need a little more information and I have to start somewhere.

Grandma's face sags even more than usual, but she forces a smile. Her eyes go instantly moist, but so far the coast is clear of full-on Grandma tears.

"I did," she says. "Same way my mama told me and her mama told her."

She pours the soupy package of strawberries and syrup into our large bowl of finely cut fruit and stirs it with an oversized wooden spoon like she's digging through quicksand.

She looks up and squints at me, forcing a single tear out of her left eye. "What made you ask about that?"

"Oh, nothing," I say, reaching down and scratching the top of Tucker's head. He moans with pleasure and then shakes out his mane when I stop, like I messed up his hair or something. Grandma scoops some fruit salad into a bowl and sets it in front of me.

"Did you ever think they were real?" I ask.

She grabs a spoon from the drying rack in the sink and hands it to me. "What's that?"

My impatience slips out in a sigh. Mama says I'm impatient sometimes and that I get that from Daddy. At least I got *something* from Daddy. Danny got everything else—his looks, being good at sports and hunting. He even got Daddy's name.

"The Whispers," I say. "Do you think they're real?"

I stare at her, filling my mouth with an overflowing spoonful of fruit salad. It's too good to eat slowly—the creaminess of the bananas, the tangy-ness of the oranges, the sweetness of the overripe peaches, the slight crunchiness of the apples, all marinating in the juicy goodness of strawberry syrup. It tastes so good it makes my jaw ache a little.

Grandma finally answers, kind of matter-of-fact. "Of course they're real."

I wipe my mouth with a paper towel and swallow down the half-chewed fruit salad. "You mean like real in the flesh? What do they look like? How big are they? Where do they live?"

She doesn't answer, her attention drawn to the stove, where a saucepan full of Lipton tea bags begins a rolling boil.

"MOTHER GOOSE NURSERY RHYMES! SOLVE! SOLVE, YOU NITWIT!"

Grandma wobbles over to the stove and moves the pan off the hot burner with a quilted pot holder protecting her hand. She's always been short and round, but lately she doesn't walk too good. Bad knees. Bad ankles. Bleeding varicose veins. You name it, Grandma's got it or had it. Grandma's what they call a hypochondriac.

A *hypochondriac* is someone who claims they have every ailment under the sun, whether they really do or not. It doesn't mean they're bad people, though. They just can't help themselves.

Of course everything got worse after Mama went missing. Before that, Grandma was pretty active. She even used to take me and Danny swimming at the community pool in Upton in the summer. Now she only leaves the house once a month to drive down to Miss Ethel's Beauty

Emporium to get her hair set and dyed, or to go to her doctor's appointments. Grandpa does all the grocery shopping now. He never gets it right, though.

I sit patiently as Grandma presses down on the tea bags with the back of a fork, squeezing out every drop of tea flavor possible.

"Mustn't be wasteful," Grandma says.

She uses the word *mustn't* when she's trying to sound proper. She always wanted to be a schoolteacher, but she was the oldest of six kids and her daddy made her quit school to help with the younger ones after her mama died.

She pours the tea from the saucepan into the pitcher, her hands shaking a little. Then she dumps in two heaping cups of sugar before adding water from the sink.

"There are starving children in Africa, you know," she adds.

Somehow I don't think Lipton iced tea is what those starving kids in Africa need the most. I guess God doesn't listen to their prayers either. But instead of saying all that, I try to get Grandma back on track. My track.

"Grandma?"

She looks at me while she stirs. "Huh, sweetie?"

I take a deep breath so my words don't come out sounding cross or disrespectful even though Daddy's impatience is percolating in my veins. "The Whispers. Have you ever seen one?"

"Well," she finally says, "I can't say I ever actually saw them."

I let out a disappointed sigh. "Then how do you know they're real?"

She turns the burner off, wobbles back over, and sits down across from me again. She looks me straight in the eyes and her face grows dark. "My mama said she saw 'em one time. Said they was ugly as sin. Small, yes, but with huge yellow, jagged teeth, horns on top of their little bald heads, and wings as sharp as razor blades."

I stare at her with my mouth hanging open. I wait for her to start laughing any minute now like she does sometimes when she's just messin' with me, but she doesn't.

"And then, of course, there're the hobgoblins." She gets up from the table, taking my empty bowl with her to the sink.

I don't think I heard her right. "The hob . . . what?"

"Hobgoblins," she says, casually rinsing out my bowl like it's perfectly normal to discuss the existence of hobgoblins with your eleven-year-old grandson. "They live in the woods, too. Big old nasty creatures. And you don't even want to know what they eat."

I can't resist. "What do they eat?"

She looks over her shoulder at me. "You just better hope you never see one, son."

I swallow hard. "Have you ever seen one of these . . . hobgoblins?"

"PRESIDENT OF THE UNITED STATES!" Grandpa yells from the den.

Grandma wipes her hands on the dish towel draped over her shoulder, her eyes growing cloudy and distant.

"Grandma?" I say.

She looks over at me and her eyes are completely glassy now. "What's that, sweetie?"

Crap.

"A hobgoblin," I say cautiously. "You were telling me about the Whispers and the hobgoblins. In the woods."

Her face wrinkles in confusion, a look I've seen from her a lot lately. She's sharp as a tack one minute and foggy the next. It's probably because of the shoe box full of pill bottles she keeps on the coffee table. We don't talk about that, even when she rummages through it right in front of God and everybody.

"Never mind," I say, not wanting to confuse her any more than she already is. "It's nothing."

She gives me a weak smile and wipes down the counter like she's wiping our conversation right out of her memory. But that word is seared into my brain.

Hobgoblin.

5

MY CONDITION

I have trouble falling asleep that night partly because I'm racking my brain again trying to remember the song, but mostly because I can't stop thinking about what Grandma said before she went foggy on me. What if a real live hobgoblin took Mama? It could have easily come out of the woods and walked right into our house. I assume they know how to open doors. Actually, I don't know anything about hobgoblins—what they look like or how big they are—but I bet they're strong. Strong enough to carry off a full-grown woman, even. Could a hobgoblin be keeping Mama somewhere in the woods? Do they live in caves, or shacks, or under bridges like trolls? The Whispers would know if a hobgoblin has Mama, that's for sure. I just have to find them.

There's a light tap on the door.

"Come in," I say, thinking it's Danny. But then again, Danny wouldn't knock.

Daddy pushes the door open a little and sticks his head in. "Just checking to see if you were asleep yet."

I shake my head, wondering if he's going to come over and tuck me in the way Mama does. He probably thinks I'm too old for a story and a song. I probably am, but that never stopped Mama.

He stays wedged in the door like this is a hospital room and he doesn't want to get too close in case I'm contagious.

"Bathroom?" he asks with question mark eyebrows.

I nod and hold up four fingers.

"Okay, then," he says, glancing at my wall of words. I know it makes him think of Mama. He looks back at me quickly with no particular expression on his face. "Get to sleep. School tomorrow."

I nod as he backs out of the open wedge of space. "Good night, Daddy."

I think I hear him say *good night* back, but the door was closing at the same time, so I can't be sure. I could've imagined it.

Seventeen words. Nineteen if you count the possible *good night*. I think he's trying.

On the floor beside my bed, Tucker groans. He's just as restless as I am tonight. I don't let him sleep with me anymore because of *my condition*. That's what Grandma calls it. *My condition*. She always lowers her voice when she says it, like it's a rare disease or something that people might catch if she says it too loud. But there's no medicine or treatment for *my condition*. Jesus can't heal me either. I already asked—a lot. Maybe the Whispers can, though. Why not hope?

I went to the bathroom four times before getting into bed even though nothing came out the last two trips. I try not to think about it, because the more I worry about wetting the bed, the more likely I am to do it.

I haven't always wet the bed. It started right after Mama went missing. Daddy didn't seem too concerned at first, but after a couple of weeks of a soaked mattress and sheets, his frustration took hold and hasn't let go. It's like every time I do it I'm reminding him that Mama's gone since I never did it before she disappeared, except when I was a baby, I guess. At first he cleaned up after me, but I couldn't take the shame of that. If I'd done it when Mama was here, she wouldn't have made me feel bad about it.

What's a little pee in your bed when so many people in the world don't know where they're going to sleep tonight, Button? I can imagine her saying, and she helped real homeless people because of her social work job, so she would know.

But Daddy couldn't hide his disgust with the smelly sheets and stained mattress. To be fair, I don't think he'd ever done laundry before Mama was taken. And no one wants to touch someone else's pee-soaked sheets, so who am I to judge? He finally broke down and bought a new mattress for my bed along with a vinyl cover that makes crunching sounds every time I roll over. I've cleaned up after myself ever since.

Unfortunately my brother knows about *my condition* too. He doesn't tease me about it, but in a way that's almost worse. Instead he looks at me like I'm some kind of alien egg hatching that he doesn't want to get too close to. If he teased me a little bit about it, that would be normal, I guess. Not that I want to be teased about anything. Especially not *my condition.*

I lie on my back trying to remember even just the melody of the song Mama used to sing to me at night. She made up the song just for me when I was born. As I got older, she would hum it instead of singing all the words because it's a lullaby and I'm not a baby anymore. But since she disappeared, I can't remember the words *or* the melody. I feel like I've failed Mama—*again*—because I can't remember it.

After a while, I give up, roll over on my side, and stare at the word wall. The moonlight slips in through partly open shades just enough that I can see most of them. Our words. The small black-and-white square slips of paper, each with a date, a word, and its exact dictionary definition. They cover a whole wall, hundreds of them, like word wallpaper. There's hardly any empty space to add new ones. It looks like a dictionary threw up in my room or something.

Way back when I turned ten, Mama got me a word-of-the-day desk calendar for my birthday because Grandpa got her and Uncle Mike one when they each turned ten. She said she got Danny one too, but I guess it didn't take, because there's nothing on his walls but posters of guns, motorcycles, and torn-out pages of *Sports Illustrated* swimsuit models. Danny doesn't know as many words as I do even though he's in high school.

The calendar sits on my nightstand because I like to

rip off the day's word before I go to bed and peek at what tomorrow's word will be so I can be ready for Mama. After we read the exact dictionary definition together, Mama explains them to me in her own words, which usually makes me laugh. Mama is real funny sometimes. Then she'll ask me to explain what it means in *my* own words, and also to use it in a sentence.

Use it in a sentence, Button, she says every single time.

Mama always says, *Know as many words as you can, but only use the words you know.*

Mama also says that people who use big words that they don't know the meaning of are puttin' on airs.

I look over at the small square calendar to remind myself what today's word is.

Petulant.

After rereading the exact dictionary definition, I decide on the *my own words* meaning.

Petulant is when someone is a pain in the butt to be around because they act like a hemorrhoidal jerk all the time.

Coming up with a sentence for that one is easy.

I feel really bad for Mama and Daddy because even after all their hard work raising us, Danny turned out to be a very petulant child.

I rip the *petulant* sheet off the calendar and lay it on the nightstand so I can tape it to the wall in the morning.

Something taps my window, drawing my attention. Like a fat bug had a head-on collision or something. I hope it wasn't a moth. They leave a mess. I lean up on my elbow and peer through the partly open shades into the darkness. I don't see anything at first. Then, out in the middle of the yard, a bluish glow catches my eye but quickly fades away. I slip out of bed and lift the shades to get a closer look. I can't really see anything, though. Just the dark outline of Daddy's work shed, the shadowy stalks of the Pentecostal corn choir, and the moonlight casting a hazy glow over the treetops in the distance. Maybe I imagined it.

I open the window a little bit. I like to hear the night crickets sing, and the birds waking up in the treetops in the morning are my alarm clock. They can make a real ruckus when the sun comes up, like angry teenagers complaining to God that they can't sleep all day long like Danny does on Saturdays. Sliding back under the still warm, dry sheets, I glance over at the nightstand and review tomorrow's word. *Feckless.*

That's going to be a tough one to use in a sentence.

I wake early the next morning, right in the middle of a dream about Mama. She was telling me the story of the Whispers before bed and she was about to sing the song, but then I woke up. At least it wasn't the nightmare I've been having lately.

I realize that I'm cold and soaking wet from the waist down. The familiar stench fills my nostrils. I shiver as I slip out of bed. Tucker lies on the rug in the center of the room, watching me with one eyebrow raised, giving me his *not again, dude* look.

I strip the bed and take off my pajamas as quickly as I can and gather the bundle of pee-smelling evidence. Tucker doesn't bother getting up with me. This has become so routine that he can't be bothered anymore. Maybe he's embarrassed for me, or by me. I'm not sure which. At least Tucker has the decency to whine by the back door until someone lets him outside to go pee. He stares at me like he doesn't understand the whole double standard of it all. Why do I get to pee in my bed when such a fuss is made about even the idea of him doing his business anywhere inside the house? He's right, of course. Tucker's always right.

I haul the whole mess down to the laundry closet in the kitchen. The house is quiet and I try to make as little noise as possible loading the washing machine, adding a capful of Tide detergent, closing the lid, and turning the noisy dials. Before Mama went missing, I'd never done a stitch of laundry in my life. I did help her with the folding, though. That's how I learned to tri-fold the towels. Not everybody does it that way, but it's *very* important to Mama. But now I'm practically a pro at the whole laundry process, from dirty towel to clean Mountain Spring–smelling tri-folded towel. If Daddy ever kicks me out of the house, I could probably get a job at one of those twenty-four-hour laundromats in Upton because I'm good at making change, too. Mama taught me that you count from the amount *owed* up to the amount *given*. It makes perfect sense once you get it. Danny still doesn't get it. Danny's not only petulant, he's not very bright.

My goal is always to have my sheets washing and a fresh set on the bed before Daddy wakes up. That seems to at least lessen the look of disappointment in his eyes. Back in my room, I close and lock the door. I spray the vinyl mattress cover with my own personal stash of 409 cleaner that I keep in the nightstand and wipe it down with a damp rag. Then I spray the whole thing with a generous helping of Lysol. I also give the room a healthy blast of the stuff and for a moment even consider spraying my whole body, just to make sure Daddy and Danny don't get a whiff of my shame at breakfast. Luckily I have time to shower before I get ready for school.

Last step in my morning routine. I reach under my pillow and pull out the sandwich-sized Ziploc bag. The word PRIVATE is written on it in black Magic Marker in big block letters. The plastic is completely dry. Thankfully the pee-tide didn't rise that high this time. I hold the bag in the palm of my hand and stare at the lone passenger inside. Mama's wedding ring. Nothing fancy—just a plain gold band. But she was always so proud of it, you'd think it belonged in a museum or something.

Daddy was Mama's first and only love, she used to say. They were childhood sweethearts. Grew up right down the road from each other when he was just Daniel

James, *daredevil–bad boy*, and she was just Carolyn Riley, *straight-A beauty queen*. Daddy never had another girlfriend his whole life and Mama never had another boyfriend.

Your daddy spent every last dime he had on it, she always says when she takes the ring off and lets me try it on. I like the way it looks on my finger. I think I'd like to have a wedding ring one day; I just don't want the girl that comes with it.

A cabinet door slams in the kitchen, a little harder than usual. Daddy's up and the running washing machine must have put him in a mood—a three-cycle reminder of his defective son. The loud buzzer at the end is always an added bonus, bringing even more attention to *my condition*. I hurry over to the dresser and slip the Ziploc bag into the bottom drawer, way in the back under my heavy winter sweater. Finally, after reading the exact dictionary meaning of *feckless* one more time, I grab *petulant* off the nightstand and tape it to an empty sliver of wall space near the window. I *should* go tape it on the door of Danny's bedroom.

While the 409 and Lysol dry, I head down the hall to the bathroom to shower off the stench of my latest disappointment.

6

JUNIOR BLACK SANTA

I've always thought Buckingham Middle School is oddly named. Sure, Buckingham is the name of the county we live in, but it's also the name of a famous castle in England. And Buckingham Middle School sure doesn't look like a castle. BMS looks like a giant cinder block with windows and only barely passes as a real school. The teachers do the best they can, but we spend most of our language arts class sitting around while Mrs. Barker tries to get half of the class up to sixth grade reading level, because Buckingham Elementary is even worse.

The second-period bell rings, announcing it's time to herd ourselves down the hall to a whole different classroom for South Carolina history with Mrs. Turner. One thing Buckingham Elementary has going for it is that the teachers there know how to teach *all* the subjects, so you stay in one classroom the whole day. I guess the teachers at BMS could only afford to learn one subject apiece—instead of moving *them* from room to room, they move all of *us*.

It doesn't seem like a very efficient system, but I don't mind the changing-classes part of middle school too much. I guess it's good practice for high school because I hear they change classes like every five minutes or something. Plus sometimes I get to see Dylan Mathews in the hall between classes even though he's in the eighth grade. He's usually alone and not very talkative, but he always gives me a little wave and smile. We're kind of neighbors. Well, neighbors with a ginormous cornfield separating our backyards. Country neighbors.

The hallway is noisier than usual. Everyone is buzzing about the long holiday weekend coming up—early dismissal tomorrow and no school on Monday because it's Labor Day. The girls are especially noisy. I'll never for the life of me understand why they have to talk so loud and how they have so much to talk about. They used to lower their voices down to whispers and stare at me when I passed them in the hall, but that was back when Mama first disappeared. Her picture was in all the newspapers back then and it was all anyone talked about for a while. *Local beauty queen*, *social worker*, and *tireless advocate for the indigent and incarcerated*, they called her in the papers. Danny cut out all the articles but he won't ever let me see them because he's a horrible person. Now everyone seems to have forgotten that there's still an open police investigation going on and that I'm the star witness.

I peer down the crowded hallway and finally spot

Gary. The eighth graders tower over him, but pretty much everyone has a hard time getting *around* him. Gary looks like he has a car tire under his shirt. He's big, but in a junior black Santa sort of way. I never knew there was a white Santa for white kids and a black Santa for black kids until Gary set me straight on the subject. Gary has a white mama and a black daddy, which is unusual in Buckingham County. Most everybody here is either all the way white or all the way black, so Gary gets called some not-so-nice names sometimes, but I think it's kind of cool that he's different. Even though Gary's technically only half black and his skin is only part the way black, he says he feels all the way black on the inside, and since I can't see what his insides look like, who am I to disagree? I wonder if both the black Santa and the white Santa visit Gary's house on Christmas. I'll have to ask him about that. It seems unfair.

He makes a beeline for me, parting a sea of thin people like bowling pins. I wait by my locker so we can walk into class together.

"What up, dawg?" Gary says. He calls me *dawg* sometimes. I don't know why, but I don't mind.

Gary grins from ear to ear. Always does. He acts like he hasn't seen me in a week even though we sit together every day on the bus. I didn't mention the Whispers to him on the ride in this morning. I'd planned to, but his little brother Carl was right there the whole time. Besides, all Gary wanted to talk about after Carl got off the bus at the Buckingham Elementary stop was Rebecca Johnson's rapidly developing chest. She must work out.

"Hey," I say, following him into Mrs. Turner's classroom after taking one last peek down the hall. No Dylan. I turn back to Gary, lean in, and lower my voice. "Meet me by mobile unit three after lunch."

Gary scrunches up his face. "Okay. But you better not try to kiss me."

My whole face goes hot and my heart thumps hard in my chest. I actually take a step back, like he just farted or something.

"What?" The classroom fills with noise and shuffling bodies. I glance around to make sure no one heard him. "Why would you say such a feckless thing?"

Feckless is when your best friend says something super dumb without thinking that other people might hear him.

Gary shrugs like he understands the word *feckless*. I can't believe he knows the exact dictionary definition like I do. Maybe I just used the word so well in my sentence that Gary understood its meaning. Mama says that's the whole point of the word-of-the-day game.

"People meet behind the mobile units to smoke and kiss," Gary says, lowering his voice. "And you don't smoke. Jesus, dude, it was a joke. Chill out."

I shoot him a glare. "I said *by*, not *behind*."

I take a desk in the back row, still a little shaken by his feckless comment. Gary knows better. But maybe he didn't mean anything by it and I'm just overreacting. Daddy says I do that sometimes.

Gary squeezes into the desk to my right. We both eye Mrs. Turner with caution because she's a real stickler about starting class precisely when the late bell rings. I wouldn't call Mrs. Turner mean, but as Gary says, *she don't play*. Mrs. Turner is strict and doesn't smile hardly ever, but she's still the prettiest teacher at school. She looks like Cassandra Bailey on *DC Fixer*, who wears those long white coats and walks real fast with her whole body swinging every which-a-way. She fixes everyone's problems in Washington, even the president's. Cassandra Bailey don't play either.

Gary's a favorite target of Mrs. Turner and usually for good reason. He says she's just hard on him because she's all the way black and he's only part the way black. But I don't think Mrs. Turner gives a crap what color Gary's skin is. He just gives her a lot to work with. But I understand why Gary might think that. He's been picked on a lot over the years for being mixed, and he says he doesn't feel like he fits in with either the black kids *or* the white kids. It's kind of how we became friends.

When I got to first grade at Buckingham Elementary, I had never seen so many other boys in one place at one time. And I liked just about every one of them I saw. White, black, brown—it didn't matter. I wanted to kiss them all. That was before I knew how the world works. It's not a good idea to try to kiss every boy you run into at the coat cubby when you're hanging up your Wonder Woman backpack. I learned that the hard way. About the kissing *and* the Wonder Woman backpack. People started calling me not-so-nice names. I was too young to really pay attention to the sermons at North Creek Church of God back then, so I really didn't know I was doing anything sinful.

Around the same time, Gary was getting a lot of questions from the other kids about his parents, and he didn't know any better than to just tell them the straight-up truth. So we both got picked on a lot those first couple of years at Buckingham Elementary. Nobody wanted to play with us at recess, so we ended up hanging out together. It was Gary who told me that maybe I shouldn't try to kiss other boys behind the coat cubby. Even though I'd never tried to kiss him, he'd heard about it. Apparently everyone had.

In third grade, Gary told me maybe it was time to trade in my Wonder Woman backpack for a Captain America or a Black Panther one. Those two pieces of advice made the rest of my life at Buckingham Elementary much easier, and I'll always be grateful to Gary for that.

Gary leans over and whispers to me before Mrs. Turner turns around to face the class. "What did you want to talk about at recess?"

"Going camping," I whisper back. The late bell rings and I look up. Mrs. Turner turns on her heel, plants a hand on her hip, and settles a steely gaze on the class—daring anyone to trespass on her time, just like the DC Fixer would. I gamble with my life on one more whispered message over to Gary.

"This weekend."

And for a second, I think about asking Mama to take me to the Walmart in Upton to get snacks for our camping trip because they have a much bigger selection than Mr. Killen's Market. Just for a second, though.

Then I remember that I can't.

7

MY OWN PERSONAL REDNECK SUPERHERO

I stand with my hands shoved deep inside my pockets and stare out over the dusty courtyard during recess. The grass has been completely worn away by the back and forth shuffling of middle school feet, and the school district can't be bothered to plant any shrubs for the poor country students. The same clumps of kids stand on their same clumps of grass, while others walk the length of the courtyard and back again like they're strolling through Central Park in New York City.

We sixth graders are the most disorganized bunch, wandering here and there and not really knowing our place. We haven't even separated ourselves by race yet like the older kids—although that'll never happen to Gary and me. The sixth graders are still changing over from actually playing at recess, like we did at Buckingham Elementary, to standing around talking, which seems to be the standard recess activity in middle school. The seventh and eighth graders are real pros at it. From what I can tell, and what

I've seen on *CID: Chicago*, it's like learning your place in a prison yard—knowing who to stick close to, who to stay away from, and who to avoid eye contact with.

I look over at Gary, leaning against the side of the mobile classroom. His belly sticks out like a human turnstile blocking entry to the private spot from intruders. I'm not sure of the best way to casually bring up magical wood creatures in regular recess conversation, so I just plow right in.

"Have you ever heard of the Whispers?"

He tears his gaze away from Rebecca Johnson, who stands with a group of girls across the courtyard, and cocks his head at me. "The what?"

"The Whispers," I say. "You know the story?"

Gary shakes his head. "Sorry. No idea what you're talking about, dawg. And what does it have to do with camping this weekend? I can bring hot dogs and buns. You get the snacks. I'll try to ditch Carl, but you know how my mom is."

He's going to think I'm crazy. Everyone else does. Maybe I am.

"It's this story my mama's told me since I was little," I say.

Gary lowers his head at the mention of Mama. It's a common response at school whenever I talk about her or bring up the investigation. It started soon after the abduction when I gave a show-and-tell presentation in Miss Diaz's social studies class on Mama's case and the police's progress (or *lack* of progress) in finding her. It was a big hit. The whole class stared at me in wonder. I had them in the palm of my hand—you could have heard a pin drop. Miss Diaz was so impressed by my presentation that she called Daddy to tell him all about it. He wasn't too thrilled, though. Neither was Frank.

I guess I overstepped the bounds of police procedure by discussing the case in public or something. Frank later told me maybe I shouldn't share any of my personal theories about what happened to Mama to anyone other than him and my family. He said it could *impede their progress*. It all felt very official. Like Frank really did care about finding Mama and that I had almost botched the case. But I don't think it was an *official* police gag order or anything. I doubt Frank has that kind of authority. Besides, I'm the star witness, so as much as Frank doesn't like it, I can say whatever I want. I think it keeps the police on their toes.

I give Gary the abridged version of the story of the Whispers.

Abridged is when you leave some stuff out of a story to make it shorter because your best friend has a hard time concentrating and can't follow regular-length stories.

When that word came up on my word-of-the-day calendar, I think back in March, and Mama told me to use it in a sentence, I said, "Grandma's favorite song is 'Abridged Over Troubled Waters.'" I thought that was a pretty good joke and it made Mama laugh real hard.

I can tell by his wrinkled face that Gary's not following me. I didn't really do the story justice the way Mama does.

"Wait, so they're like magic birds, or flying fairies, or what?" he says when I reach the end.

"I don't know what they are exactly," I say honestly. "But I think they can help me find my mama."

Gary gives me the side-eye and then does the head lowering thing again. "It's been how long now? Four months? You still think she's coming back, dawg?"

Before I can answer, the worst human person in the history of human persons appears in front of us like he was conjured out of thin air. And *conjured* would be the perfect word to describe the sudden appearance of the Voldemort of Buckingham Middle School. Apparently Gene Grimes and his posse of supercharged puberty mutants, Chad Wells and Jack Toomey, were hanging out behind the mobile unit, probably smoking. And listening.

"What was that about finding your mommy?" Gene says with that sneer most of the seventh graders have when they talk to sixth graders. "And fairies?"

Gene, Chad, and Jack snicker and play-punch each other in the arm like idiots. Danny would fit right in with these losers. Gary rolls his eyes but keeps his mouth shut. Gene stands a good foot and a half taller than both of us. It's a known fact around school that he works out. He has actual biceps, which he shows off by rolling the sleeves of his polo shirts up over his shoulders at recess all the time, even on days when it's not very hot out, like today. Chad and Jack have biceps too, or at least the beginnings of biceps. And supposedly they all drink beer and smoke cigarettes after school every day, so they're going to hell anyway. They'll have all of eternity to work out there. That's what the preacher at the North Creek Church of God says about drunks and fornicators. Unless they repent, hell is in their future.

Repenting is when you're super sorry about something and promise Jesus you'll never do it again, even though you know you probably will.

As in, *Gene Grimes doesn't seem like the repenting sort, so you know, hell-bound.*

"Your mommy's gone, turd breath," Gene says, hocking a loogie on the ground in front of me. "And there's only one fairy around here."

He pokes me in the chest with his index finger, just to make sure I understand what he's saying. I do. My cheeks heat instantly. That's the second mention today of *my other condition.* I'm beginning to wonder if someone put a sign on my back when I got off the bus this morning.

"The police are still looking for her," I say weakly.

Gene curses under his breath and gets in my face so my nose fills up with his skanky breath. Definitely smoking. "Well, why don't you just tell them where she is, you wack-job?"

My breath catches in my throat and I clench my teeth so hard they just might break off in my mouth. I don't know if I'm more angry or shocked. I know Frank has his suspicions about me, that's becoming pretty clear. And maybe even Daddy does too. But do people at school think I had something to do with Mama's disappearance?

Gene starts making a lot of wild and crazy accusations about what happened to Mama, like he's Detective Chase Cooper or something, so I tune him out. Internal Charlie Brown teacher translator activated.

. . . wah waah wah wah, waah wah waah . . .

As Gene blathers on, the only two things I can think to do to shut him up are to punch him or vomit on him. I've never thrown a punch in my life, so Gene's pretty safe there. But I've vomited *a lot* in my life. I'm kind of a pro at it. I look over at Gary for help but he just stands there with his head down, no doubt hoping Gene will keep his psychoness directed at me. *Thanks a lot, buddy.*

"Leave him alone." A voice—loud, clear, and deep— comes from behind Gene, sounding not like Charlie Brown's teacher at all, but like the voice of Jesus. Or Superman.

I peer over Gene's shoulder and I'm instantly filled with hope, relief, and a stomach full of butterflies—but not the vomiting kind. Gene steps back and turns to face Dylan Mathews. They're roughly the same size, but Dylan came by his muscles honestly—working his family's farm and tending their cornfield behind our house. He's wearing a red Peterbilt ball cap, faded jeans with worn holes in the knees, and a blue T-shirt with Captain America's shield on the front. So not exactly Superman, but still like my own personal redneck superhero. My face flushes hot because *my other condition* usually acts up whenever Dylan is around.

Gene scowls at Dylan, but that's about it. Dylan is in the eighth grade. Top of the middle school food chain. Gene knows his place. Besides, nobody messes with Dylan Mathews. Too mysterious. Too unpredictable. He was held back a year, so he's the oldest kid at BMS. I don't think he even has any friends, because he's always alone.

Gene looks back at me and hocks another loogie on the ground about an inch from my right sneaker. "Morbid little freak."

Gene and his supercharged puberty mutant posse stalk away, leaving me and my coward of a best friend standing there with Redneck Superhero Dylan Mathews.

"Thanks," I manage to get out, but my voice sounds a lot higher than usual. Like Lois Lane or something.

I clear my throat. Dylan doesn't say anything. He just looks me up and down with an expression I can't read. Maybe he believes the things Gene says about me. Maybe Gene has been saying those things to everybody ever since I tried to kiss him behind the coat cubby at Buckingham Elementary when I was in first grade and Gene was in second. Anyway, I'd hoped Gene had forgotten about that. I guess not.

"What was that about?" Dylan finally says in a low mumble. He slips his hands into his pockets, pushing his scuffed jeans down low on his waist. His deeply tanned arms are long and have all these hills and valleys dented into them. I know he doesn't have one of those redneck tans that only show on his face, neck, and arms, because I've seen him working in the cornfield without his shirt on. I try not to stare at him from my bedroom window when he's out there driving the tractor around, but I can't help it. So I repent. A lot.

"Gene heard Riley talking about trying to find his mama," Gary says, jumping in when I fail to answer.

The two of them share a look that bothers me. I get why Dylan might think I'm crazy for believing there's still a chance the police will find Mama. The whole town has given up on finding her. They don't even write about her in the newspapers anymore. But Gary is my best friend. And a traitor, apparently.

"Don't pay Gene no mind," Dylan says to me, glancing over his shoulder toward the courtyard. He's probably hoping none of the other eighth graders see him talking to us sixth grade peons. "He's just a spineless bully."

"Hey, Dyl," Gary says. For some reason he doesn't get as flustered as I do talking to Dylan. He even dares to *abridge* Dylan's name. "Have you ever heard a story about the Whispers?"

Traitor times two.

"It's just a dumb bedtime story my mama used to tell me," I say, jumping in, downplaying Gary's bigmouthed confession. I can't believe he's embarrassing me in front of Redneck Superhero Dylan Mathews like this. "You know, before she . . ."

I hate using the word *disappeared*. Mama didn't just *disappear* into thin air. She was taken. Abducted. Kidnapped. That much I know. I can't prove it, but I just know it in my gut. Something about the suspicious car that was parked in the driveway that day and the shifty-looking guys who were sitting in it watching the house. But the police have come up empty-handed—no leads, no suspects, no ransom note or call. And I know what some people think—that Mama left of her own free will. They don't understand that Mama would *never* do that to me. Not possible. Not even after that Kenny from Kentucky dude showed up and ruined everything.

"I've heard it," Dylan says, saving me from my tongue-tied state. "The story about the Whispers. My grandma used to tell it to me when I was a kid."

I stand there staring up at him. I don't know what to say. I've never known anyone else who's heard the story outside of my family. I thought it was something passed down to my mama from Grandma, and her mama before that.

The way Dylan stares at me makes me nervous. Like he's looking right through my eyeballs into my brain and knows all my secrets that I keep hidden back there.

That I wet the bed.

That I have no interest in Rebecca Johnson's miraculously inflated boobs.

That I have Mama's ring.

That I stare at him through my bedroom window when he's working in the cornfield without a shirt.

I feel like I'm going to vomit right on his Captain America T-shirt.

"Do you think they're real?" I manage to squeak out vomit-free.

The bell rings before my own personal redneck superhero can answer.

8

GIANT YELLOW DEATH BOX

Even though I still haven't forgiven him for making me look stupid in front of Dylan at recess, I sit with Gary on the bus ride home that day. His little brother Carl gets on at the Buckingham Elementary stop and sits in the seat in front of us, watching and listening to everything we say. Carl favors their white mama more while Gary favors their black daddy, but Gary says that Carl is just as black as he is on the inside, so who am I to argue? Besides, Mama says God is color-blind even though most people aren't, but that we should try to be more like God than most people. Makes sense to me.

Carl doesn't talk much. He seems perfectly happy letting Gary be the big brother and control everything, including their conversations. I'm glad my brother has to ride a different bus now that he has to go all the way into Upton. That's where the closest high school is. Buckingham throws in the towel on its kids after they graduate from middle school. After that, you get yourself to Upton if you require further education.

Miss Betty weaves the bus down the dusty back roads of Buckingham, fishtailing slightly every few minutes. The windows rattle in their frames like alarms going off, pleading with her to slow the heck down. Miss Betty is an old black lady who always wears a pink-and-blue housecoat over her day dress, and sandals that barely contain her crusty biscuits. She's a retired nurse and way too old to be driving forty schoolchildren in a giant yellow death box this close to a six-foot-deep ditch. Her Coke-bottle glasses do nothing to calm our nerves.

As Gary rambles on about Rebecca Johnson's butt, or chest, or one of her other rapidly developing body parts, I casually glance over my shoulder. Dylan Mathews sits in his usual seat in the back row. Alone. Sometimes I wonder if he's embarrassed to be trapped on here with a bunch of kids when he should really be on the Upton High School bus. He's slumped down in the seat, so only the top of his straw-colored hair is showing. It's always buzzed short, which somehow makes him look even older than he really is.

"Be right back," I say, cutting Gary off. I have to do this before I chicken out.

I pop up out of my seat and wobble down the aisle to the back of the bus, grabbing on to seat corners to steady myself as I go and hoping we don't get any closer to that ditch.

"Riley James," Miss Betty barks from up front.

I glance back over my shoulder at her. She narrows her eyes on me in the oversized rearview mirror.

"Sit yo' narrow behind down, boy!" she yells.

"Yes, ma'am," I call over my shoulder and hurry the rest of the way to the back. Miss Betty has the unusual talent of switching on a dime from being the sweetest old lady you could ever meet—*mornin', baby, bye, sweetie, tell ya mama and 'em Miss Betty said how ya durin'*—to the most terrifying. Like announcing to the whole bus how narrow (or wide) your butt is, or how if she wasn't busy driving the bus she'd give you the *tail whoopin'* your parents are too *lily-livered* to give you. It seems really unprofessional, but no one's going to tattle on Miss Betty. Not when our lives are completely in her hands for an hour a day, five days a week.

When I reach Dylan, I realize his eyes are closed. His head bobs around a little, following the jerky movements of the bus. I ease backward, but his eyes pop open.

"Sorry," I say. "I didn't know you were sleeping."

He scratches the back of his head and stretches his arms out wide. His T-shirt rides up, exposing a tanned sliver of smooth skin, and just like that, my cheeks go hot. I look away so he doesn't think I'm some kind of hell-bound pervert or something.

When he scoots up in the seat, he winces a little and touches his side. "It's okay," he says, playing it off with a weak smile. "What's up?"

I sit facing him on the edge of the empty seat across the aisle and will my voice not to fail me like it did at recess.

"I just wanted to say thanks for what you did today," I say, impressed by the sturdiness of my voice. "With Gene."

Dylan shrugs. "Let me know if he bothers you again."

My insides melt into a puddle of goo, but all I do is nod.

"And just forget that stuff Gene said about your mama," he says, leaning his head back on the seat and looking me straight in the eye. "I bet you'll find her real soon."

His words are so kind and unexpected that if I don't just ignore them, I might lose the tiny bit of cool I've managed to pull together. If I tear up in front of my own personal redneck superhero, I will never forgive myself. I keep going before my tongue reties itself into a knot.

"Have you ever *heard* them?" I say. "The Whispers?"

He closes his eyes and laces his fingers together, resting them on his flat stomach. "Nope. Can't say I have."

I feel like an undercover cop, inspecting his face while his eyes are closed. His skin is golden brown and his cheeks have a deep red glow. A few—*seven*—light freckles dot his nose, but otherwise, his skin is smooth and flawless. Not that Dylan's seven freckles could be called flaws, really. His jaw is firmly set and he has what Mama calls *cheekbones for days*.

Dylan either senses my disappointment in his answer or my pervy inspection of him, because he opens one eye and grins a little. "But that don't mean they ain't real." He closes the one eye again. That's when I notice for the first time how long his eyelashes are. He gives his lips a casual lick that aggravates *my other condition.*

The bus hits a deep rut in the road, jostling everyone in their seats. Dylan opens his eyes and glances out the window, probably to see how close we got to the ditch and our death. I feel like I'm intruding on his nap, and being a little creepy too. He probably has to get right to work on the farm when he gets home.

"We're going camping tomorrow after school," I say, trying to drag out my time with him as long as possible without seeming like a stalker.

Stalking is when you can't stop thinking about someone, so you break into their house and watch them while they sleep, or make up excuses to be close to them when they're awake. It's a real crime. They made a whole show about it, but it got canceled after only one season.

As in, *I could be breaking the stalking law right this minute, but hopefully Dylan wouldn't press charges against me because he's a nice person.*

"So if you're out there hunting, don't shoot us, okay?" I stand to leave, pleased with my small attempt at humor. But Dylan doesn't smile. His face actually goes a little dark.

"Y'all need to watch yourselves when you go out there," he says in a serious tone. "Stay close to the tree line. All kinds of crazy in them woods."

His dark brown eyes plow into mine, like he knows something I don't and really wants me to hear his warning.

We only go deep into the woods when we're exploring during the daylight. We *always* stay close to the tree line when we go camping. But that's not the plan this time, and he looks at me like he knows that.

I nod. "Okay." I turn and head back down the aisle to my seat while Miss Betty isn't looking, Dylan's words needling me the whole way.

All kinds of crazy in them woods.

9

CAN'T NEVER COULD AND
IF NEVER WOULD

Later that afternoon, I count down the minutes until the sun sets. I try distracting myself with homework and then with chores. I'm allowed to go into Danny's room without his permission even though he's not home from football practice yet because I'm on trash duty this week. Danny has *a lot* of trash.

I push right through his door like I own the place. *Ugh. What a dump.* There're underarm-smelling clothes all over the floor. The trash can is overflowing with wadded-up tissues. He must have a cold. Game magazines cover the bed. It's a mess. But I'm sure Daddy thinks it's better than a tidy room with pee-soaked sheets.

My eyes are drawn to one of the magazines on the bed, so I pick it up. On the cover is a shirtless brown-skinned man in tight black pants with tons of muscles bulging out every which-a-way. He's holding some kind of huge space machine gun, and beside him the headline says:

Cord Stargazer Is Back!

It's just an avatar and not a real live man, but *my other*

condition starts acting up anyway. I quickly put the magazine back where I found it and shake those thoughts out of my head. That's when I notice the corner of a white book sticking out from under Danny's bed. I look over my shoulder even though no one is home, because I know I shouldn't be snooping. All clear. Dropping to my knees, I slide the book out slowly and recognize it right away. It's one of our family photo albums from back when people still had photos printed at the Walmart and then put them in spiral-bound albums. We used to have four or five of them on the bookshelf in the living room, all full up to the brim with our memories, but I haven't seen them since Mama went missing. I figured Daddy took them down to the police station so Frank and his team would have lots of different pictures of Mama for their search. Turns out Danny kept one for himself.

I open the album and right there on the first page is a picture of me and Mama sitting on the back porch swing, except I'm really little. I remember this one. I'm sitting in her lap and she's tickling me. I probably peed on her. There's a bunch of other pictures too. One of Mama and Daddy getting married at the North Creek Church of God. They don't look much older than Danny is now. Another one of Mama's and my last joint birthday party, when she got strawberry cake with white and red icing and I got yellow layer cake with chocolate icing. There's another picture of me and Danny with Grandma and Grandpa one Easter all dressed up for church and standing out in front of Mama's climbing red roses on the front porch. One shows me and Danny when we were little, sitting in front of the Christmas tree in matching blue and black cowboy outfits. Danny sits cross-legged and wears a cowboy hat. I sit with my legs folded under me. I don't have on a cowboy hat like Danny's. I was probably afraid it would mess up my hair or something.

There're a lot of pictures of Danny when he was a baby—way more than there are of me when I was a baby. I guess that's because he got here first and Mama and Daddy were more excited about him being born than me. Plus everyone talks about how Danny was so beautiful when he was little that some people thought he was a girl. Nobody thought I was a girl, though. When I was a baby, I was bald and fat and not very photogenic.

Photogenic is when some people look really good in just about every picture they take, no matter what kind of face they're making, what they're wearing, or how horrible of a person they are.

Like, *My brother is very photogenic on the outside, but if someone took a picture of his heart, I bet it would be all shriveled up and dead.*

I flip through a few more pages and stop when I spot one of my favorite pictures ever. It's from the Christmas parade years ago, right after Mama won the Mrs. Upton pageant. She's sitting on top of the back seat of an open silver Mustang convertible in a pretty blue dress with a little white hat and long white gloves like Cassandra Bailey wears on *The DC Fixer*. On the side of the car is a sign that says Mama is sponsored by Daniel James—Independent Contractor. Mama looks like a queen waving to the crowd. But she wasn't waving to just anyone when this picture was taken. She was looking right into the camera and waving at me. I remember like it was yesterday. I waved back, which is why the picture is a little blurry. I was so proud my mama was *the* Mrs. Upton that I couldn't stay very still. And I was probably too young to be taking pictures of a beauty pageant queen anyway, so not my fault.

A door slams down the hall. I snap the photo album closed and stuff it back under Danny's bed, but something blocks it. I lean down to see what it is and find four other family photo albums stuffed under there. Danny stole them all.

Heart dead as a doornail.

We eat supper at Grandma's house that evening. The windows are open because it's not nearly as hot out tonight as it's been lately. It's the last day of August and it's like September is giving us a little taste of the weather it will bring. A honeysuckle-scented breeze rolls in over the dining room table, cooling our food and reminding me that it's almost time.

Grandpa and Daddy sit at each end of the table. Danny and I sit across from each other. He doesn't like to sit beside me because he says I smell like pee and Lysol. I promise I don't, though. I'm a little nervous about that part of the camping trip. But Gary and I usually stay up all night talking, laughing, and stoking the fire. As long as I don't fall asleep, I should be okay.

I still have to get permission to "stay over at Gary's house." After a local boy named Peetie Munn went missing a while back, Daddy didn't want me to go camping with Gary in the woods anymore, but Mama would say it's okay as long as we stayed close to the tree line, so I'd always ask her for permission and not him. The police arrested Mordecai Mathews for the Peetie Munn thing, but they couldn't ever prove he was guilty. Nobody's seen or heard from Mordecai since they let him go. Most people think he's dead, so I'm not scared. Besides, Daddy doesn't seem to care too much about what I do and where I go these days, anyway.

Grandma seems to be in decent spirits tonight and her mind a little sharper than it's been lately. She's sitting between Daddy and me, probably on purpose, but she doesn't eat anything. She never eats with us, just cooks and cooks and cooks and then sits there watching us eat and refilling our plates. Or, if she has one of her sick headaches, she might lie on the sofa in the living room, take some medicine, and pass out while we eat. Mama says that Grandma knows how to cook everything under the sun except a salad. Tonight she made fried pork chops, green beans, stewed potatoes, and a box of Kraft macaroni and cheese. The mac and cheese is always just for me. Danny doesn't like it. He only likes the homemade kind. His loss.

I don't talk much at the table because I don't want

supper to go long and miss being outside when the sun goes down. Mama always says that's the best time to hear the Whispers—as day turns into night, when your senses are a little slippery and the colors of the sky and the sound of nature's symphony all kind of melt together. Mama calls that *magic time.*

Grandma tries to replenish my unnaturally orange and unnaturally delicious mac and cheese, but I hold my hands over my plate. "No, thank you. I'm full."

"Full?" she says. "You're a growing boy. You need to eat."

"No, really, Grandma," I say. "I'm good."

She eyes me suspiciously but sets the bowl back on the table. She's always trying to give me extra. Extra food, extra money, extra attention. She understands how hard Mama's disappearance has been on me. What's a mama's boy without his mama, anyway? A grandma's boy? It's not the same.

"They say it's cloudy tomorrow," Grandpa says down the table to Daddy.

Daddy nods and glances up at Grandpa. "Clear the weekend, though."

That's it. Eyes back on his plate. That's usually about how their conversations go lately. That one actually went on a little longer than usual.

"Frank called today," Daddy says in a low grumble. "He wants to talk to you about something tomorrow afternoon."

Exactly thirteen words. It's the first and only thing Daddy's said to me since he got home from work, and even though he doesn't look at me when he says it, everyone knows it was directed at me. The whole table goes silent. Like he just told me I have a date with the devil. Frank's a little slow and a terrible police detective, but he's hardly the devil.

"Why do I have to go back so soon?" I try and fail to keep the whine out of my voice. Daddy doesn't like it when I whine. He says I'm getting too old for *that junk*. "I've given him my statement like a hundred times," I say. "I told him I don't remember anything else. He should spend his time trying to find Mama instead of harassing me."

Daddy lifts his head and looks at me. His eyes are cold and go dark on a dime.

"If Frank says he needs to talk to you, you will go and you will talk to him," he says, gritting his teeth, his eyes piercing. "And you will tell him the truth. Every blasted bit of it."

He slaps his hand down on the table. Hard. I jump a little in my seat. Everyone stops eating mid-chew and freezes. Danny and Grandpa both look up from their food at the same time, staring back and forth from Daddy to me. Grandma shifts nervously in her seat beside me and clears her throat. At my feet, Tucker lets out a soft, throaty growl of his own. Daddy's not the least bit threatened by the show of aggression from my protector, but anyone else would be.

"I always tell him the truth." I immediately regret opening my mouth. Daddy purses his lips and forces a steady stream of air out his nose. He rubs his hands over his face and then flexes his fingers, like he's trying to keep them from forming into fists.

I sit frozen in my chair, afraid to move an inch. Since Mama was taken, Daddy has been distant, but he's never been cruel. It wasn't even so much what he said as the way he said it. And his meaning was clear. He thinks I know more about what happened to Mama than I'm telling. But I don't. I promise.

Daddy hangs his head and covers his face with his hands. "I . . . I can't. I just can't anymore."

He doesn't say it to anyone in particular, but I know it's meant for me. He probably means he can't love me anymore.

Daddy keeps talking—about Mama, about Frank—but I don't hear him. It all gets dumped into my internal Charlie Brown teacher translator.

. . . *wah waah wah wah, waah wah waah* . . .

Plus all I can think about is the fact that he just used *that* word. There're two words that we're forbidden to use. *Can't* and *if*.

A couple of years ago, Mama and Daddy decided they were sick and tired of me and Danny making excuses for everything. Like when Daddy tried to teach me to catch a football and I kept saying I *can't* do it every time the darn thing hit me in the chest. Or when Danny would say he'd make better grades *if* his teachers liked him. Mama would always respond by saying, "*Can't* never could and *if* never would!" That got real annoying, *real* fast.

One day Mama made us empty out two plastic containers of washing detergent and decorate them like little people. She gave us yarn to glue on top of the containers like hair. Mama's crafty. I used extra yarn on mine to make a mustache. We drew on mouths, glued on buttons for noses, and used Mama's old dishrags to make little coats for them. They turned out pretty good for what we had to work with, and we actually had fun doing it together.

With a black Magic Marker, Mama wrote *Can't* on the front of one of the laundry detergent people, and *If* on the other. While we were busy decorating *Can't* and *If*, Daddy was outside digging two small rectangle holes in the backyard by the old oak tree. He also made two simple wooden crosses with sticks that were planted in the ground at the end of each mini grave with *Can't RIP* written on one and *If RIP* written on the other. We had a funeral out in the backyard that day. Me, Danny, Daddy, Mama, and Tucker. And with *Can't* and *If* dead and buried, Mama said we're never allowed to use those words again. Mama's been real strict about it, even after Tucker dug them up a week later and chewed them to bits. But Daddy just said *can't*. Twice. It's like he's just given up on everything—even Mama's rules.

"Who wants dessert?" Grandma says, creating a diversion.

A *diversion* is when something bad is happening, so someone waves their hands in the air and yells, "Hey, stop looking at the bad thing that's happening and look over here!"

As in, *I wish Tucker would create another one of his farting diversions so I can slip out before the sun sets.*

Grandma touches Daddy's arm gently. "Daniel? How about some fruit salad?"

She knows he can't resist her fruit salad. No one can.

Daddy takes a deep breath and exhales slowly. The muscles in his face relax a little and he gives her a quick nod. "Sure."

Grandma's fruit salad saves the day. Again.

Daddy doesn't look at me and I don't say another word to draw his attention. He used to like me. He used to like me a lot, actually. He used to kiss me on the cheek every day before he went to work and hug me every night before I went to bed. I mean, Danny has always been the daddy's boy in our family, sure, but I never minded because I had Mama. I don't know where I fit in now that she's not here. I'm like an annoying stray cat that won't go away because someone keeps feeding it. What's a mama's boy anyway without his mama? Nothing, that's what.

That's why I have to find the Whispers. They'll know where to find Mama. I have to take matters into my own hands, solve this case, and find her before something terrible happens to her.

Or before the police find out what I did and arrest me.

10

MAGIC TIME

Daddy says I can ride my bike for a little while after supper. I think he feels bad for yelling at me and for saying *can't*. I take advantage of his guilt and go ahead and secure his permission for this weekend's "sleepover at Gary's" too.

Secure is when you lock something down so you know it's a sure thing.

As in, *Gary's trying to secure a date with Rebecca Johnson for the school dance, but it'd be a miracle if Rebecca Johnson even knows Gary is a live human person.*

I stand there in the backyard, straddling my bike and gazing past the cornfield to the tree line of the woods. Tucker sits on his haunches beside me—ears pointed up to Jesus and eyes alert, like he's listening for them too. We wait patiently as the wind picks up and the golden sun dips below the tree line in super slow motion. Nature's symphony has already started its nightly concert. That's what Mama calls the evening song of the crickets, frogs, cicadas, and birds— *nature's symphony*. I listen carefully, wishing with all my heart and mind that the Whispers would speak to me. I know I'm running out of time. *She's* running out of time. And I just can't imagine a world without Mama in it.

"Please," I say in a whisper of my own. "Please help me find my mama."

Tucker cocks his big Rottie head at me, giving me his *dude, are you talking to yourself again?* look.

I remember something from the story and turn my face back into the full force of the wind.

"I have gifts for you," I say, hoping the breeze will carry my message and deliver it to the Whispers.

"Tributes," I clarify, using the word for *gift* from the story. "Really good ones, too."

I listen. Tucker listens. I wait. He waits. Nothing but nature's symphony and the wind sounding like ocean waves in my ears. After a few minutes of nothing, I sigh and look over at Tucker.

"What do you think, Tuck? You think I'm crazy?"

He cradles a soft whine in the back of his throat. I'm pretty sure that means, *sorry, dude, but pretty much.*

I look back to the tree line. "I don't think I'm crazy. I think you're real. And I need you to help me find her."

Nothing. I stare at the slowly dimming woods a moment more, watching the wind roll through the treetops like the human wave people do in the stands at football games. I close my eyes. A wind chime sounds in the distance as the warm breeze slips over and around my face, changing directions on a dime. It brushes my cheeks and the soothing scent of honeysuckle tickles my nose.

I try to imagine what their voices would sound like calling my name. Would they even sound like voices at all? Would they sound like a human person? Or an animal? I will myself to hear them, but still, nothing. Frustrated, I let out a deep sigh, open my eyes, and lift the handlebars to turn my bike around.

"Come on, Tuck."

As I'm pushing away from the spot, something buzzes my right ear—something bigger than a fly. A wasp? A horsefly? I duck and swat at it. A small blue trail of light flashes in front of my face, but fades away just as quickly as it came—just like outside my window last night. My breath catches in my throat, and that's when I hear it. I swear to Jesus and all his disciples, including Judas, I hear it. My name—gently tucked in the folds of a honeysuckle breeze.

Riley.

I freeze. Every muscle in my body tenses up. I know I heard it. I'm sure I did. My heart thumps so hard in my chest I'm afraid the noise of it will scare them away. Tucker slowly rises up on all fours, a low growl rumbling in the back of his throat. He heard it too. Either I'm *not* crazy, or we both are.

"Easy, boy," I say, hoping he doesn't spook them. "Shhhh."

I gaze out into the dusky twilight, inching my bike toward the edge of the yard. It came from the tree line beyond the cornfield, I'm sure of it. But it's also like the voice—or voices—tickled the rims of my ears. Like they were out there and right here all at the same time. It was like nothing I've ever heard before. One voice, but also many. Far away, but close up too. A sudden gust of wind whips the Pentecostal corn choir into a Holy Ghost frenzy. The treetops in the distance sway like they're waving me forward, testifying that the Whispers are out there somewhere, just waiting for me to come find them.

Riley.

There it goes again—soft and barely there. Far away and yet right in my ear. I push off and start pedaling. Tucker trots ahead of my bike, leading me down the dirt path lining the Mathewses' cornfield. I don't go too fast or pedal too hard. I need to figure out exactly where the voices are coming from. It sounds like they're everywhere, filling every dark shadow of the woods. But there has to be a central location, like a Whispers ground zero or something. A clearing with a rotted-out tree stump, like in the story.

Now that the sun has disappeared, night comes quickly, making everything around me gray and dim. It feels like there're a million eyes watching me from the shadows of the woods—some of them friendly, but some of them, maybe not.

I look over my shoulder just to make sure the nonmagic world I know is still back there. The rooftop of our house and Grandma and Grandpa's beside it are small in the half-lit distance over the cornfield, but at least I can still see them. I look forward again and slow my pedaling to a complete stop. Resting my feet on the ground, I steady the bike between my legs and listen. The tree line in front of me is like a dark fortress. Something about it in this magic time light screams *DO NOT ENTER*. Too many shadows. Like the big one moving closer to me right now, just beyond the fortress walls. I watch as the slow lumbering form stops just ahead, staying hidden behind a row of tree trunks. Tucker spots it too and growls at it.

Riley.

It doesn't shock me this time, but I can hardly contain the excitement of hearing my name echoing through the woods and yet somehow right in my ear. I wonder if the giant shadow is like a Whispers hive or something, and they've come to greet me—to carry me right on in to see Mama. But the shadow monster is gone now, vanished into thin air, and I can still hear them. I guess it wasn't a Whispers hive after all. Maybe it was a ginormous deer. Or the ghost of Mordecai Mathews. Or Bigfoot.

The breathy voices seem to be coming from the right of where the sun disappeared. North. That's one of the things Gary and I learned exploring these woods in the safety of nonmagical daylight—which-a-way is which. I walk my bike over to the tree line in that direction. Tucker stays right beside me—the fur along his spine rising and a growl thickening in his throat. I'm glad he's here because I haven't forgotten for a second about the other dangers lurking out in the woods at night, and I don't just mean bobcats and coyotes.

Hobgoblins.

I ease my bike to the ground and creep closer to the tree line on foot. The voices sound again, not as clear this time, but definitely coming from the north.

Something buzzes my head again and a faint bluish glow forms a path in front of me, like it's leading me into the woods. But as soon as I focus my eyes on it, it fades into darkness.

Tucker lets out an anxious whine and gazes up at me, his big brown eyes pleading. I know he wants to bolt into the woods right now and chase them. So do I. But Dylan's words shuffle around in my brain.

All kinds of crazy in them woods.

Still, I take a step forward, crossing over the shadow border.

"Riley? Riley!" Daddy's distant voice echoes over the cornfield, sharp and irritated. Out here in the country, a father's angry tone carries for miles and vibrates deep in your bones.

Tomorrow is Friday. I can wait one more day. I'll be more prepared and I'll have some good backup in Gary. I pull Tucker from the tree line by his collar. He's a little stubborn about it but doesn't fight me. Lifting my bike upright, I hop on it and peer into the shadowy woods once more. I can't see much of anything, but I know they're out there. Watching me. Waiting for me.

"I'll be back," I whisper to them.

I push off toward the house with Tucker trotting close by my side. Even as I ride away, I hear them calling out to me. Their voices simmer in the hazy stew of twilight and come to a quick rolling boil, like the Whispers are upset that I'm leaving. But one last message slips through the garbled soup of white noise. It rides the swell of nature's symphony, tickles the rim of my ear, and warms me from head to toe.

She's here.

11

A GOSSIP

The next morning I wake so full of anticipation that the whole day is a blur of routine.

Pee-soaked sheets in the washer.

409.

Lysol.

Put clean sheets on the bed.

Hide the ring under my heavy winter sweater in the bottom drawer of my dresser.

Tape feckless on my wall. (Have to stand on my desk to reach a clear spot for it.)

Review the word of the day—cavernous.

Avoid Daddy.

The short school day passes in a blur, too.

Language arts.

South Carolina history. (We learn about the Swamp Fox. The real human person, not the roller coaster in Myrtle Beach.)

Gene Grimes calling me a freak and a princess in the hallway between classes. (That second one is new.)

Math.

Early dismissal.

The only two things that really stick out are that Miss Betty let out a string of R-rated curse words when she clipped and destroyed a mailbox on the bus ride home, and Dylan Mathews wasn't at school today. Maybe he didn't come because his family is going away for the holiday weekend or something. But I can't spend time worrying about why Dylan skipped school because I finally have a lead on Mama.

A *lead* is a piece of information that could help you solve the case.

As in, *Frank probably couldn't find a lead if it slapped him upside the head.*

But the Whispers said Mama was out there in the woods somewhere. That's a *solid* lead. Maybe she hasn't been eaten by a hobgoblin after all. Or maybe the Whispers know where the hobgoblin is holding her hostage. Or maybe they've been protecting her all this time. All I know is that I'm going to find them so I can find her.

Before I get off the bus, I tell Gary to meet me at our usual spot at the tree line at five thirty. I should be back from what I hope is my last interview at the police station in plenty of time for us to find somewhere good to set up camp before the sun goes down. Tucker meets me in the driveway and gives my hand a couple of *welcome home, dude, glad you survived another day at that nuthouse* licks. Tucker gets it.

Grandpa is heading into Daddy's work shed, but he doesn't see me. I haven't gone into Daddy's work shed since the Kenny from Kentucky incident, but I squash that memory right out of my mind before it can take hold. That kid is bad news. I drop my backpack on the steps of the porch and head straight over to Grandma's house. I find her sitting at the kitchen table riffling through her shoe box of prescription pills with her reading glasses clinging for dear life to the end of her nose.

"Hey, sweetie," she says, distantly lost in her search. Then she mumbles, "Migraine. Blood pressure. Heart. Arthritis—"

"Hey, Grandma," I say and jump right in with the bait . . . or lies. "I'm staying over at Gary's house, so I'm going down to Mr. Killen's to get snacks to take with me. His mama never has anything good. You need anything while I'm there?" Not all lies. It's good to sprinkle in some truth. I *am* going to get snacks, and Gary's mom *does* buy mostly fruits and vegetables as snacks. Like that makes any sense.

Grandma looks up at me, her eyes a little glazed over. She must have already found her Xanax. That's a pill you take to make you feel fluffy. But Grandma says I won't need it anytime soon.

"Some Crisco," Grandma says. "The big tub. Go grab me my pocketbook off the coffee table."

Bingo!

I do as I'm told, and when I return, Grandma digs through the bag. She practically has her whole head in there.

"Grandma," I say. "I don't know how in the world you find anything in that *cavernous* bag of yours."

It was the perfect use of today's word, but she barely

notices it, so lost in her search. If Mama were here, I know she would've laughed at my sentence using the word of the day. Grandma finally pulls out two bills—a twenty for the Crisco and a ten for me.

"Don't tell anybody," she says in a near whisper as she wads the ten-dollar bill and presses it into my palm like this is a drug deal or something.

I thank her with a hug and meet Tucker in the backyard. He and Grandpa are playing tug-of-war with a stick. Tucker is winning. I use the same line on Grandpa, and while he doesn't add anything to my shopping list, he slips me a five-dollar bill with the same cloak-and-dagger routine that Grandma did. Grandpa's usually a little cheaper than Grandma, but I can always count on both of them. Detective Chase Cooper on *CID: Chicago* might call this extortion.

Extortion is when you shake people down for money by making threats against them. But in my defense, Grandma and Grandpa *want* to give me money and I don't ever threaten them. They just need an excuse, so that's what I give them.

Like, *The way I get money from my grandparents by supplying them with excuses to give it to me is really more of a public service than extortion.*

"Be back soon so I can take you to your . . . your . . ."

Grandpa never knows what to call my trips down to the police station.

"It's called a voluntary police interview," I call out,

pushing my bike toward the road with Tucker lagging behind. His game with Grandpa plumb wore him out.

Tucker waits by the front door of Mr. Killen's Market like a huge, furry security guard. Even though he's lost some weight since Mama disappeared because he hasn't been eating as much, he's still over a hundred pounds and pretty scary looking to most people. We took him to the vet when he started throwing up his food. The doctor thought it might be his pancreas and gave him some medicine. That helped for a little while. I just think his heart is heavy right now. I can relate—without the throwing-up part. My heart feels like it weighs a ton these days.

Mr. Killen is helping a customer in the sporting goods department. That's what he calls the ammo counter in the back of the store. He waves at me as I pick up a basket and start grabbing everything we need for the camping trip.

Matches. *Check.*

Two cans of Vienna sausages. *Check.*

Two six-packs of Mountain Dew. *Check.*

Family-size bag of Ruffles. *Check.*

Two bags of Mr. Killen's World Famous Boiled Peanuts. *Check.*

A bag of Flamin' Hot Funyuns. *Check.* Actually, those always give Gary explosive farts, and we'll have a fire. I put them back and grab the plain ones.

"Well. If it isn't Riley James."

I look up from my Funyuns and find Sister Grimes, mother of the Voldemort of Buckingham Middle School, looking down her nose at me. Sister Grimes is not a nun. She's a member of the North Creek Church of God and the adults there say *Brother* and *Sister* instead of *Mr.* and *Mrs.* It's a little weird, but no one there ever called me *Brother* anything, so who am I to judge?

"We sure do miss you and your father and brother at church," she says, though she's looking at me like I have leprosy or something.

Leprosy is a really gnarly disease they had a lot back in Bible times where you got sores all over your body and nobody wanted to get anywhere near you.

As in, *As far as I know, Jesus is the only cure for leprosy.*

I just nod at her. I don't like this woman at all, and not just because she gave birth to Satan's baby and named him Gene. Sister Grimes is a gossip. That's what Mama calls her. *A gossip.* Which sounds way worse than just being someone *who* gossips, like Grandma.

I haven't seen Sister Grimes since the last all-day singin' and dinner on the ground at the North Creek Church of God. I overheard her saying something about my mama that day. I never told anyone, and honestly right now I can't remember exactly what it was she said, but I remember thinking it was horrible at the time. I haven't forgiven Sister Grimes for gossiping about Mama. Jesus says we're supposed to forgive, but I don't think I ever will, so I hope Jesus isn't sitting around waiting to hear from me on that.

I stand there holding my basket in front of me and staring at her. I've heard that it makes adults uncomfortable when children respond to them with a silent, blank stare. And that it's rude. And creepy. I don't care. I want Sister Grimes to be uncomfortable and creeped out. And I want to be rude to her because of what she said about Mama. If only I could remember what it was.

My plan works. She finally gives up waiting for me to say something and just rolls her eyes a little as she passes me. "Well, tell your father I asked about him."

Yeah. That's not going to happen.

I give her the creepy kid stare until she disappears around the corner, just in case she looks back. She doesn't. I continue my shopping and get all the way to the end of the snack aisle before I find myself at the ammo counter in back and face-to-face with Redneck Superhero Dylan Mathews. I stop dead in my tracks and stand there staring at his face. And not just because it's Dylan Mathews's face—which is usually a good enough reason alone to stare at it—but also because his upper lip is busted. It's swollen with a little dried blood caked on it. Who in the world would have the guts to bust Dylan Mathews's lip?

"Dylan," I kind of blurt out, like he may have forgotten his own name and needs reminding.

He looks at me wide-eyed, as if I caught him doing something illegal. But I can't stop staring at his fat lip. That is until the purple-and-brown bruise on the right side of his jaw catches my attention. *Holy crap.* I think it, but I don't dare say it.

Mr. Killen glances at Dylan and then flashes me an annoyed look. "Finding everything you need, Riley?"

Dylan looks down, not able to hold my gaze for some reason. I want to ask him what happened to his face, but Mr. Killen's one raised eyebrow warns me not to and I don't want to be nosy like a gossip would.

"Crisco," I finally say. "Grandma needs Crisco." My mouth is suddenly bone-dry and the words come out sounding like scraps of sandpaper.

"The big tub?" Mr. Killen asks.

I nod, still staring at the bruise on the side of Dylan's face. Mr. Killen walks out from behind the ammo counter with a sigh, I assume to go get the Crisco because I can't seem to move my feet from this spot to go get it myself. I wonder if Gene Grimes and his supercharged puberty mutant posse jumped Dylan in retaliation for him taking up for me. But Dylan wasn't at school today, so I don't know when that would have happened. He rests his hands on the counter. They're shaking a little. He still hasn't said hello to me, which is strange. Dylan always says hello to me, or at least he waves.

Two boxes of shotgun shells sit on the counter in front of him. He stares at them as if he's silently briefing them on their mission, like Detective Chase Cooper would instruct his team before he leads them through the door of the perp's hideout.

"You going hunting?" I manage to get out.

He glances over at me. "Something like that."

I want so badly to know what happened to his face— who did that to him, and was it the reason he wasn't in school today. But the strange combination of rage and fear in his eyes rattles me away from the subject.

"Why ain't you in school?" he asks.

"Early dismissal," I say.

He nods a little like he remembers now. I guess his family isn't going away this weekend after all, or he would've known that.

"Me and Gary are going camping," I say, for lack of anything better.

He nods once and looks down at the boxes of shells again. "That's what you said on the bus."

"Oh. Yeah, right."

I glance around and spot Mr. Killen waving a tub of lard at me. Sister Grimes watches me from the dairy case like a gossip would.

"If that's all, Riley, I can check you out up front," Mr. Killen says, his voice louder than needed for the amount of space between us. "I'll be right with you, Dylan."

Dylan nods over his shoulder at Mr. Killen.

"We're going north of the tree line behind your dad's cornfield," I say. "So don't shoot us out there."

My lame joke doesn't go over any better than it did on the bus. Dylan doesn't laugh. He doesn't even smile. So I just wave at him and turn to leave.

"Be careful out there, Riley." His voice is small and tight behind me like a little kid's—not a superhero's.

I look over my shoulder, but he's standing with his back to me. I guess it wasn't an invitation to keep talking to him. Even though he can't see me, I nod and leave him there alone with his dark thoughts, his bruises, and his shotgun shells.

12

COP WORD OF THE DAY

Fat Bald Detective blows his nose again. He tries to stifle the noise, but it sounds like he just blew half his brains out—and believe me, Frank can't afford to lose any brains. I look away as he turns to grab another tissue. My gaze lands on a couple of framed certificates hanging on the wall. They look official enough, I reckon. One is probably a high school diploma. Frank probably *did* finish high school, but I doubt the other one is for college. Frank's not smart enough for college. Maybe it's his certificate of completion for his online detective course. Or a commendation.

A *commendation* is like a pat on the back, but on paper.

Like, *Frank could've received a commendation for trying really hard, but being a total disappointment as a detective.*

I can't stop squirming in my seat on his Fritos-smelling couch. I'm nervous because I was just here. I wonder why Frank wanted to see me again so soon. Did he somehow find out about the ring? Or about Kenny from Kentucky? But how could he? No, that can't be it. Maybe he heard I was discussing the case at school again. Or he somehow knows I have a solid lead that I'm not sharing with him. Is that obstruction of justice? Not that he would believe me anyway.

Hey ya, Frank. Just thought you should know that there are magical creatures in the woods who talk to me and they know where my mama is. So thanks for all you've done (cough, cough—not), but I got this now.

No, that probably wouldn't go over so well. After a couple of minutes waiting for him to finish spreading his germs all over the place, he spins around in his chair to face me. He casually wipes his hand on his pants leg like he's brushing away lint or something.

We both know it isn't lint, Frank.

"Sorry about that," Frank says. "Allergies."

I wonder what Frank is allergic to. Probably dieting and solving cases.

"Thanks for coming in again so soon, Riley. I just wanted to follow up on something from our last talk."

Frank thinks if he calls our meetings *talks* and not *interrogations*, which is what they are, that I'll relax enough to slip up. He has a little notebook and a pen resting in his lap this time—finally. I wouldn't have to keep coming down here and repeating myself if he'd been taking notes all along. We could have saved the taxpayers a boatload of money. I sit there and don't say anything. Just wait for him to go on. Why should I help him do his job? He needs all the practice he can get.

"You asked me if we'd found their car," Frank says and then stares me down with that annoying plastic smile of his. "*Their* car."

I stare back at him for a silent moment, my mind racing, retracing every word I said the last time I was here. "I did?"

My voice is scratchy and I kind of stutter out the words. Even *I* think I sound guilty. Beads of sweat instantly form around the collar of my shirt. My heart starts thumping Frank a message using Morse code or something. I don't know Morse code, so I don't know what my heart is trying to tell Frank. Maybe my heart thinks I'm hiding something too and is ratting me out. My heart could be Frank's CI—a *criminal informant*. But that would mean my heart is a criminal. And a blabbermouth. Sounds about right.

"Yes, you did," he says, casually crossing his legs knee over knee. That's what they do on the cop shows on TV when they think they're getting somewhere with their interrogation of the perp. They sit back and casually cross their legs like they've figured something out and have you cornered. Or at least that's what they want you to think. Detective Chase Cooper does it all the time. It's usually a trap.

"It's just that you've never mentioned there being more than one person who took your mother."

"I didn't say for sure that—that someone took her," I say, stammering a little. I don't know why he's rattling me this way.

I don't know anything. "I said I don't remember. I just assume someone did. What else could have happened to her?"

He'd better not say that she left of her own free will, or I might just turn into the murderous lunatic everyone seems to think I am.

"So the last time we spoke, why did you give the impression that there may have been more than one . . . culprit?"

He says the word *culprit* like it's a new one for him. They use that word all the time on the cop shows on TV. Maybe Frank's mama got him a cop-word-of-the-day desk calendar since I last saw him. But I'm starting to get super nervous. I wonder if it shows. I try to stay calm and keep my face blank.

Stick to your story, I tell myself. *Stick to your story and everything will be fine.*

I take a deep breath, lean forward, and give Frank that same hard look that Dylan gave Gene Grimes at recess yesterday. "Are you charging me with a crime, Detective?"

Frank raises his eyebrows and smiles. "Detective? What happened to just Frank? No need to get so defensive all of a sudden, Riley. I'm your friend. I'm trying to help you."

That's how they get you. Make you think they're on your side to get you talking. Maybe Frank's trying the old good cop/bad cop routine and he's playing the part of the good cop. A scarier detective will probably bust into the room any minute now and start screaming in my face. But I'm not playing along.

"Help me how?" I say, feeling annoyed. "By trying to trick me into saying something I don't mean? Incriminate myself? Trying to entrap me? Shouldn't my daddy be here for this? Or my lawyer?"

Entrap and *incriminate* are also words they use a lot on the cop shows on TV. But I can see by the confused look on Frank's face that he probably hasn't gotten to the *entrap* or *incriminate* days on his cop-word-of-the-day desk calendar yet. And I don't even have a lawyer, but it may be time to get one. I wonder how much they cost and if Grandma and Grandpa would slip me enough fives and tens to pay for one.

"Okay, Riley. Take it easy." Frank leans forward, patting my knee. "You said you didn't want your father in here for our talks. You insisted, actually. And I'm only repeating what you said for clarification so I can help you remember more about that day."

I can see it in Frank's Mr. Potato Head smile. He still thinks I know more than I'm telling. This might be how police brutality starts, because I have an uncontrollable urge to slap him right across his fleshy face. But then he'd probably throw me in one of those holding cells, unplug the camera, and rough me up with his bad-cop partner. Then I'd miss my chance to find the Whispers tonight. And Mama. And to clear myself. Better dial it back a notch so I can get the heck out of here in one piece.

"Sorry, Frank," I say, making my tone friendlier. "I was just confused again. I might have said *their* white car last time, but if I did, I don't remember why. Probably just a slip of the tongue."

Frank nods and scribbles something in his shiny new notebook.

"What are you writing?" I ask, sounding way guiltier than I mean to.

Frank looks up with a satisfied smile stretching across his face. He holds up the notebook and flips it around so I can see what he wrote.

WHITE car.

My heart, the snitch, starts sending Frank another secret Morse code message at lightning speed. Did I say *white*? I did. I said *white*. What the heck is wrong with me? This is all Kenny from Kentucky's fault. Something told me I should stay away from that kid.

"That's very good, Riley," Frank says. "See, you remember more than you think you do. You've never mentioned the color of the car before. Now you say it was white. This is good. We're making progress. I bet you'll remember even more soon."

He looks so pleased with himself and I just want to vomit. Does Frank think that I know who took Mama? Or that I was somehow in on it? That I helped those guys get away or something? Why the heck would I ever do that?

The world's worst police detective should go flip through his cop-word-of-the-day desk calendar and learn another police term he obviously doesn't understand.

Motive.

Because I don't have one.

"Mama, what's a motive?"

Mama stuffs a handful of popcorn in her mouth and passes me the bowl. CID: Chicago *just went to commercial and left Detective Chase Cooper searching for a motive for a suspect.*

"Well, let's see," Mama says after chewing most of the popcorn in her mouth. A few pieces spill out the sides, but I know she's doing that on purpose to make me laugh. It always works. "A motive is the reason why people do what they do."

"Use it in a sentence, Mama," I say, even though Detective Chase Cooper has used the word like a hundred times in this episode. I just want to see more popcorn spill out of her mouth.

She tosses back another big handful and squints at the ceiling as she chews loudly. "My motive for sending your daddy and brother to the movies tonight was so that I could spend time with Button, getting caught up on our favorite show."

Popcorn goes everywhere because she said every word with her mouth open real wide. We both laugh so hard that she chokes a little and an unpopped kernel shoots out of her nose. Then we really go crazy laughing.

Best. Motive. Ever.

13

BLACK PANTHER VS. CAPTAIN AMERICA

The house is quiet when I get home. Danny got out of school early today too, but he's probably over at one of his high school friends' houses smoking the devil's weed if Grandma's suspicions are correct. He's been extra secretive and shifty the last few months. Daddy isn't home from work either, so there's no one to see me off on my quest to find Mama. But they just think I'm going over to Gary's house, so my departure is no big deal to them. If they only knew.

I throw everything into my Black Panther backpack—a change of clothes, all the snacks I got from Mr. Killen's store, the matches, extra socks, my flashlight. I go over to the dresser and freeze when I spot the Ziploc bag with Mama's wedding ring sitting on top of it. Just sitting there out in the open in front of God and everybody. I stare at it a second, giving my brain time to catch up with my eyeballs. I know I put the ring in the bottom drawer under my heavy winter sweater this morning. I would never leave it lying out like this. At least I'm *pretty* sure I put it away. It's part of my morning routine.

I pick up the Ziploc bag and stare at the ring inside, confused. The hair on the back of my neck prickles to attention. I spin around because it feels like someone is watching me. The room is empty, but the window is open a few inches. I thought I closed it before I left for school this morning. I walk over, push it down all the way, and lock it. Maybe someone was trying to steal Mama's ring and I walked in on them and scared them away. But that doesn't make any sense because nobody knows I have it, much less where I hide it. The Whispers would know, though. They know everything. All the secrets of the universe—including where I hide Mama's ring. I wonder if they're trying to tell me something. Maybe they want me to bring the ring. Maybe the ring is like Cinderella's slipper. Like I have to take it with me and have Mama try it on so the Whispers know she's mine before they'll let me bring her home.

I shake my head. Maybe I *am* losing it after all. But Mama always says that it's better to be safe than sorry, so I stuff the Ziploc bag down into the left front pocket of my jeans just in case I'm not totally crazy.

Before I leave my room, I rip *cavernous* off my word-of-the-day desk calendar, tape it on the wall near the floor, and check out tomorrow's word since I won't be here.

Winsome.

I study the exact dictionary meaning and tuck it back in my brain for use in a good sentence later.

Before I head out the back door, I spot something on the kitchen table. A note and a ten-dollar bill. I walk over, pick up the scrap of paper, and read it.

> *Pitch in if Gary's mom buys a pizza or something.*
> *Love,*
> *Dad*

I stare at the note. Mostly at the word *love*. I know it must have been hard for him to write that. But he probably thought it would have looked bad *not* to write it, or if he wrote something like *sincerely* or *best wishes*, or nothing at all. He really didn't have a choice. I'm sure he thought about it, though. Why else would he sign it *Dad* instead of *Daddy*, which is the only thing I've ever called him?

I grab the ten-dollar bill and the note and stuff them into my pocket. There's just one last thing to get before I leave. I head over to Grandma's house and tell Tucker to wait on the back porch while I slip through the kitchen door. I don't really have a good plan. I just hope Grandma and Grandpa are napping in front of the TV like they usually do this time every day before the evening news comes on. I hear voices in the den and peek around the corner. Some old black-and-white Western movie plays on the TV. Grandpa has watched every black-and-white Western movie in the history of black-and-white Western movies. Grandma snores softly on the couch and Grandpa's in his recliner fading in and out. He'll never hear me, though, and Grandma can sleep through anything other than a turkey timer.

I tiptoe down the hall to their bedroom. The floor creaks a little, but not enough to alert them to an intruder. In their bedroom, I go over to the cedar box on top of Grandpa's chest of drawers, open it, and pull out the Swiss Army knife. He'll never know it's gone because it only comes out when I visit. I slip it into the right front pocket of my jeans. Retracing my steps, I peek into the den once more on my way out. A commercial plays on the TV now—in color. It's one of those ads about some kind of pill men take that all of a sudden makes them want to kiss their wife or girlfriend. A beautiful woman and a handsome older man run through a meadow of wildflowers and then stop to make out. It looks like they're trying to eat each other's face off. I kissed somebody once. I hope it didn't look like that. Probably not, because I didn't take the kissing pill. I glance over at Grandma and Grandpa. They haven't moved and Grandpa's completely out now. I'm better at breaking and entering than I thought. No wonder people suspect me of major crimes.

I'm out the back door with the knife in under five minutes. With a full backpack weighing down my shoulders and a rolled-up sleeping bag tucked under my arm, I set out for the woods. It's too much stuff to take on my bike, so I walk. Tucker trots at a steady pace ahead of me, but stops, sits, and stares back at me every couple of minutes, letting me catch up. He seems anxious to move me along for some reason.

"Slow down, Tuck," I say.

Like the obedient dog he is, he stays by my side the rest of the way, but complains with a high-pitched whine in the back of his throat. I reach down to touch his head, worried about him being so out of sorts lately. One night last week I found him sitting outside in the rain, just staring out at the cornfield. Tucker doesn't like the rain, at all. It was creepy. Now I wonder if he heard the Whispers before I did, because hearing things people can't is one of Tucker's superpowers. Or maybe he senses something bad is coming and he's helpless to stop it or protect me from it. Dog persons are smart like that, way more than human persons. And Tucker's usually right about everything. But this time, I hope he's wrong.

When I'm about halfway down the dirt path by the Mathewses' cornfield, the roar of a tractor sounds in the distance. I imagine Dylan sitting on top of it wearing only his jeans, his work boots, and his Peterbilt ball cap. Suddenly *my other condition* starts acting up, sparking a tingling sensation down south of my belt buckle. The preacher at North Creek Church of God said those kinds of thoughts would bring me nothing but trouble in one of his fiery sermons about sins of the flesh. I don't know if he was talking directly to me, but it sure did feel like it.

At least I don't have to sit through those kinds of sermons anymore, my face red hot and my butt numb from the hard wooden pews. Maybe the devil is slowly taking over my soul. I've prayed for God to fix *my other condition* for a long time, but He hasn't. I don't know why He won't heal me. Maybe when He hears me praying, he turns on his internal Charlie Brown teacher translator, too. I try to shake the image of shirtless Dylan out of my sinful brain by remembering his busted lip, his bruised cheek, and the darkness in his eyes at Mr. Killen's store. That does the trick.

The rumble of the tractor grows louder as it heads in my direction, but the low-hanging afternoon sun blocks my view with a blinding glare. Just when I think I'm about to get a glimpse of my own personal redneck superhero, I see that it's not Dylan driving the tractor, but his father. Mr. Mathews is a hard, crusty man. Leathery skin creases his face, and his palms are so rough and callused, people say it's like shaking hands with a brick. He's the kind of man who probably thinks my father is less of one because we live on Grandpa's land for free. But that's just because Grandpa wanted his family close, not because Daddy is some kind of freeloader or something.

As the tractor nears, Mr. Mathews looks my way, but he doesn't wave. As best I can tell, he actually kind of scowls at me and makes a hard left, guiding the tractor back toward his farm. Daddy may not like me very much anymore, but I'd choose him for a father any day of the week over Mr. Mathews.

I spot them waiting at the tree line and I'm more than a little ticked that Gary brought Carl along. I'd rather not have to worry about looking out for a whiny little kid when I'm about to embark on the greatest adventure of my life and become the hero of our family and all of Buckingham, South Carolina, by finding Mama after everyone else failed—like Frank. I guess Gary expected my disappointment because he shrugs as I approach them.

"My mom made me bring him," Gary says, nodding over to Carl.

Tucker sniffs Gary's belly like he can smell the gobs of food stored in there and then goes over to Carl. He lets the kid hug and kiss him on the side of his head. Tucker licks Carl's face and then lies down at his feet for a rest. *Traitor.*

"You better keep up," I say to Carl with as much authority as I can fake. "This is an important mission we're on this weekend. You might see and hear things that you don't understand and I don't want you freaking out and ruining it for us." Well, ruining it for me.

"I won't," Carl says with an obvious whine in his tone. That's strike one.

I look over at Gary. "Let's go in over there." I point north.

"Why there?"

I glance at Carl, not sure how much Gary told him about our mission.

"Because I think *they're* that way."

"They who?" Carl asks.

I guess Gary didn't tell him much after all. Gary ignores his little brother's question and heads off north. Carl follows him, and Tucker and I bring up the rear. Gary's pretty loaded up, carrying both his and Carl's sleeping bags, and a big backpack overflowing with groceries hanging on one shoulder. There's probably enough food in there for a week. Gary eats a lot when we go camping. I think he goes into survival mode or something, afraid that if he doesn't eat the whole family-size bag of Funyuns in one sitting, he'll wither up and die out in the woods.

Carl has a smaller Batman backpack and carries a boxed tent that we only ever use if it rains. We like to sleep out in the open by the fire. But I can't fall asleep. I didn't bring my 409, or my Lysol, not that they would do any good anyway. They don't make rubber sheets or vinyl covers for sleeping bags. I just have to stay awake for two nights straight. That shouldn't be a big deal.

Gary leads us north through the woods for I don't know how long—probably an hour or so. The light peeking through the treetops dims a little more every few minutes, so I stay alert, watching everything that moves. I don't really know this part of the woods very well and it feels a little creepy—like a-hundred-sets-of-eyes-following-us-every-step-of-the-way creepy. Maybe it's my imagination, or just squirrels who haven't crossed Danny's path yet, or deer standing frozen, blending in with the foliage as we pass. Or maybe it's something else. Some other kind of creatures watching us—like the Whispers, like the giant shadow monster I saw last night. Or hobgoblins. I'll feel better once we stop and build our fire. I remember from fairy tales I've heard that trolls are afraid of fire, and I guess trolls and hobgoblins are the same kind of thing. Probably like creature cousins or something.

"I'm tired," Carl whines. "When are we going to stop?"

That's strike two and we're just getting started.

"Shut it, Carl," Gary barks over his shoulder as he plows ahead, clearing brush and weaving us through an obstacle course of pine trees.

Gary knows I want to set up camp deeper in the woods than we usually go, but he probably didn't explain that to Carl. But we have to stop soon, before the sun sets and all the light is gone. Tucker is slowing down. He needs rest and water. I brought his food, if he'll eat it.

Gary finally finds a clear path, which makes our going a little easier.

"Superman or Iron Man?" Gary shouts out.

It's a game we play—pitting superheroes against one another and choosing who'd win in a fight.

"Iron Man," Carl shouts back.

"Superman," I say. "Without the suit, Iron Man is just

a regular guy. Superman has alien superpowers. He would destroy Iron Man."

"Wonder Woman or Black Widow?" Gary asks.

"Wonder Woman," I call out. Nobody challenges me.

"Black Panther or Captain America?" Gary says, kicking a branch out of his way.

"Captain America," I say without missing a beat. "Captain America is the man."

Gary looks over his shoulder at me with a furrowed brow and my cheeks flush hot. I didn't think Gary would remember the Captain America T-shirt Dylan wore the other day at school, but maybe he does.

"Since when do you choose anyone over Black Panther, dawg?" he says. "You're even carrying a Black Panther backpack."

I just shrug in response, clearing my mind of any thoughts of Dylan so it doesn't show on my face. Tucker sprints forward, making a beeline for a creek ahead. He laps up the water and doesn't stop until we reach him.

Gary looks around the clearing and up at the dimming sky. "This good?"

I inspect the area and nod to him. Carl drops to his knees dramatically like he just crossed the Sahara desert. He pulls out a bottle of water from his backpack and downs it in one long, messy swig. It runs all down his neck and onto his T-shirt.

Tucker sniffs around our campsite. He seems happy

enough with the choice, especially the endless supply of fresh creek water he continues to sample at different points along the bank—trying to find the tastiest spot, I guess. Gary and I shed our gear and spread out to gather wood for a fire while Carl sits on a rock panting and just watching us. That kid is useless.

I don't venture too far away from the campsite. This part of the woods has an eerie feel to it. A thick collection of soaring pines block what's left of the fading sunlight. It's quiet, but not in a peaceful way. More like in a we're-not-alone-out-here kind of way. And the path we stumbled onto earlier continues deeper into the woods. I wonder where it goes. I wonder if Mama could have walked that very path. Or maybe she was dragged down it. A stab of panic pierces my side and the urge to call out for her overtakes me.

I cup my hands around my mouth. "Mama!"

The echo of my cracking voice sails through the woods, bouncing from tree to tree. But there's no response. I really didn't think there would be. I guess I just hoped it would be that simple. That she would hear me and holler back. When I turn to face Gary and Carl, they're both staring at me. Even Tucker sits on his haunches at Gary's side, his head cocked curiously at me with his *seriously, dude?* look on his face.

"What?" I say with a sharp edge in my voice that I didn't mean to put there.

Gary shakes his head a little and starts clearing a spot

for the fire. I don't think he meant for me to see the head-shake thing. It was quick, like he forgot his manners for a second. I guess he thinks I'm crazy too. Crazy to think I hear magical wood creatures that can lead me to Mama. Yeah. I'm pretty sure that's what Gary thinks, because I saw the look in his eyes before he turned away. It was something like sympathy.

Sympathy is when someone thinks you're a total loser, so they feel sorry for you.

As in, *I don't need Gary's sympathy because I'm going to find the Whispers, and they're going to help me find Mama.*

I mean, why not hope?

14

LISTEN, WHITTLE, AND WAIT

In no time flat, Gary gets a pretty good fire going. He tends it with the concentration of a TV surgeon, adding sticks in carefully chosen spots on his teepee of burning wood. Carl sits on a tree stump, rummaging through Gary's bag looking for something. I sit on a log as long as one of the pews at North Creek Church of God, whittling down the end of a stick into a sharp point with Grandpa's Swiss Army knife. I don't know what I plan to stab with it, but it seems like the smart thing to do. If nothing else, I can use it to roast hot dogs over the fire. Tucker lies at my feet napping. I reach down and scratch his head. He's so worn out he doesn't even open his eyes.

The sun is setting, so it must be around seven thirty. Soon Gary's fire will be our only source of light. Shadows form and surround our campsite like oddly shaped doors of darkness that can't lead anywhere good. It shouldn't be long now. If I could hear the Whispers all the way at our house, surely I'll be able to hear them loud and clear out here. I listen, whittle, and wait. Listen, whittle, and wait.

At least a half hour passes and the only thing I hear is nature's symphony. They sound even better this deep in the woods. But other than that, there's no wind. No voices. No Whispers. I get up and pace around our campsite, peering into the darkness. Tucker gives up following me around after about three laps. He probably got dizzy because I'm just walking in circles, rubbing my hands together like the friction will somehow draw the Whispers out. Worry settles in my gut like a whole bag of Flamin' Hot Funyuns. Where are they? What did I do wrong? Should I have come alone?

Listen, whittle, and wait, I tell myself. *Listen, whittle, and wait.*

Gary and Carl sit on our log pew by the fire, gazing into the flames, with no idea of all the crazy thoughts running through my head. This camping trip is no different from any other to them and they both have winsome smiles on their faces, like they don't have a care in the world.

Winsome is when you think something is pleasant and fun.

As in, *Gary could stare at Rebecca Johnson's winsome boobs all day long.*

Gary holds a stick over the fire with a limp wiener dangling from the end. Carl does the same with a fireball of a marshmallow. I guess we're eating supper now. I'm not the least bit hungry, but I join them on the log pew anyway, sitting with my hands crammed down into my pockets, one cupping the Swiss Army knife, the other holding on to Mama's ring.

"Maybe we scared them away with all our racket," Gary finally says.

It's nice of him to say. He knows how disappointed I am. "Maybe."

"Scared who away?" Carl says, blowing the flame of his marshmallow out.

Gary looks over at me. I shrug and roll my eyes, giving him permission.

"Dawg's looking for something," Gary says. "And it looks like we ain't finding it tonight. Maybe we'll have better luck tomorrow."

"What're you looking for?" Carl asks me. He has ashy white goo smeared across his mouth.

I look at him a moment before I answer. Obviously they're not coming tonight, so what's the harm? "They're called the Whispers."

Carl wipes his mouth with the back of his hand. "What are they?"

"I don't know exactly," I say, feeling irritated at him for asking. "Maybe nothing. Maybe it's all in my head."

I hate that I just said that out loud, but I do wonder, and it stops Carl from asking more questions about the Whispers. I pull the Swiss Army knife back out of my pocket to work on my spear.

Listen, whittle, and wait.

Carl looks at me, licking his fingers. "Can I use your knife to sharpen my stick?"

I eye Carl's gooey fingers.

"Yeah," I say. "But go wash your hands first."

Carl pops up off the log pew, causing Gary to lose his balance, but he manages a good save before he bites it on the ground. Tucker stirs and lifts his head, watching Carl walk over to the creek. It's gotten so dark over there, I can barely see his outline bending down in the glow cast by the fire. Tucker watches him closely. He gets anxious when he can't keep an eye on all three of us at once.

Listen, whittle, and wait.

Carl splashes his hands in the water and wipes them on his T-shirt. Tucker eases up on all fours beside me and his ears point straight up to Jesus. He stares into the dark void on the other side of the creek.

I reach over and scratch the top of his head. "What is it, Tuck?"

The hair all along his spine rises and a low growl rumbles in his throat.

"Probably just a deer," Gary says, not bothered enough to look away from his flaming wiener.

The snap of a branch somewhere out there in the darkness draws our attention. Even Gary looks over. I grab my makeshift spear in one hand and grip the Swiss Army knife with the other. Gary stands slowly. He walks a few steps toward the creek bank and peers across it into the shadowy woods. Tucker's growl is steady and building, like a freight train getting closer and closer.

"I don't see anything," Gary says, turning and walking back. "Like I said, probably just a deer."

But when Gary sits down on the log pew, unblocking my line of sight, I just about fall over backward. Tucker leaps forward and darts for the bank of the creek, barking and snarling like a wild animal. Carl screams, trips, and scampers away from the creek on all fours. When I shoot up off the log pew, Gary loses his balance and actually does fall over backward. I stare straight ahead and wipe smoke out of my eyes that isn't even there, just to make sure I see what I think I'm seeing.

Standing on the other side of the creek, framed by a cape of dark shadows, is a hulking creature standing twice as tall as any of us. The flickering reflection of our fire only gives hints of the creature's face, most of which seems to be covered in hair. Lots and lots of hair. And those eyes— peering at us like two gator eyeballs floating on the surface of the swamp.

Gary scrambles to his feet, a string of curses flying out of his mouth. Carl's scream echoes through the shadowy maze of pine trees. Me? I can't move. I can't scream. I just stand there staring at the creature. The only thing separating us from its hairy clutches is the creek, and I'm sure the thing could cross the creek if it weren't for Tucker's menacing back and forth patrolling on our side. He barks, snaps, growls, and jumps up and down like he wants to rip the monster to shreds.

Carl stumbles back and knocks into my legs. "What is that?" he yells.

I stare into those beady gator eyes bearing down on me, and the word catches in my throat. I barely get it out in a whisper.

"Hobgoblin."

15

THE HOBGOBLIN VS. THE KING OF THE REDNECK SUPERHEROES

My crazed guard dog and the creek separating us from the creature keep me from turning tail right that second and running home, screaming like a banshee. That and the possibility that this thing could be holding Mama captive somewhere out here in the woods keep me anchored to the ground. I hold out my Swiss Army knife and make a great show of extending the larger blade. Gary picks up a thick branch and holds it over his head like a baseball bat. Carl cowers behind us. *Useless.*

We stand our ground—me, Gary, and Tucker. The hobgoblin doesn't move either. It's a standoff, just like on the cop shows on TV. If only Detective Chase Cooper were here. New sounds echo behind me—the rustle of crunching leaves underfoot followed by the jarring pump action of a loaded shotgun. My heart races. Maybe there's more than one hobgoblin. And they have guns. We're surrounded. We all spin around, Carl with a gasp and me and Gary holding our weapons over our heads, ready to strike the hobgoblin's accomplice.

Dylan Mathews stands a few feet away, the flames of our fire flickering across his recently damaged face like war paint. A backpack and a rolled-up sleeping bag sit at his feet, and the butt of his shotgun rests against his shoulder. He points the barrel directly at the hobgoblin. I can barely breathe at the sight of him. My own personal redneck superhero steps forward, parting us like Moses parting the Red Sea. He doesn't even glance our way, so laser-focused is he on his hobgobliny target. He walks right up to the edge of the creek beside Tucker, who instantly decides he's an ally and not another threat. Dylan has that way about him, and Tucker has always been a great judge of character.

"Mordie," Dylan says in a raised but steady tone, silencing Tucker's bark. "Get on out of here, now. Just turn around and walk away."

The hobgoblin stands motionless, training its beady gator eyes on Dylan. Tucker growls a warning for the thing to obey Dylan's command. Still, it doesn't move.

"I mean it, Mordie," Dylan calls out, taking another step forward. "Go on home now."

The hobgoblin stares at him. A few tense seconds tick by before the thing slowly backs away, never taking its eyes off Dylan. Finally, the creature disappears completely into the shadows of the woods. Dylan lowers his shotgun and stares out into the darkness where the thing just vanished into thin air.

"Holy crap!" Gary exclaims, a little too loud. "That was *insane*!"

Tucker returns to my side, panting to high heaven. I stare at the back of Dylan's straw-colored head until he turns around and looks at us. The bruise on his cheek is a little less noticeable in the shifting firelight, and though the caked blood is gone, his lip is still swollen.

"What the heck was that thing?" Gary says, pacing around the fire with the energy of a thin person.

"Hobgoblin," I say before I can stop myself.

Dylan squints at me. "Hobgoblin?" He shakes his head and chuckles under his breath, causing my face to heat from the inside out. He goes over to his backpack. Squatting down with his knees spread apart, he picks up his Peterbilt cap from the ground and slips it on. He pulls out a bottle of water and gulps the whole thing down.

"Y'all shouldn't be way out here," Dylan says, looking up at me, panting a little. He sounds like an adult, scolding us.

I glance down at his open backpack. Ours are filled with snacks and soda, but Dylan's looks like it's stuffed to the gills with clothes, like he's going on a trip or something. When he catches me staring at it, he closes the flap quickly.

"What are *you* doing way out here?" I say boldly, although I don't think I've ever been so happy to see someone in my entire life.

"Hunting," he says. "But y'all are so loud you scared off all the friggin' deer."

I nod to his backpack full of clothes and his sleeping

bag. "How long were you planning on hunting?" The sharp look he shoots me shuts me up. It's the same look Daddy gives me sometimes.

As he stands, I look him up and down. In jeans, a white T-shirt under a light camo field jacket, and hiking boots, I guess he could pass for a hunter. But it's kind of late and dark to be out hunting deer. Something seems fishy. But honestly why he's here isn't the most important thing at the moment.

"You called that thing Mordie," I say.

He nods, like it's no big deal for hobgoblins to have human person names or that he knows one personally.

"Mordecai Mathews," he says. "He's my dad's cousin."

My heart responds to the name with a hard thump against my chest.

"That was Mordecai *Freaking* Mathews?" Gary says, stepping forward. "I thought he was dead."

I did too. Grandma used to call Mordecai Mathews a *ne'er-do-well* and a *no-good-for-nothing drunk*. Most people thought he was strange but harmless—up until Peetie Munn went missing a couple of years ago. I never knew Peetie. He was a little younger than me and homeschooled. I remember people whispering about how Mordecai Mathews did something bad to the kid. But after the world's worst police department let him go, Mordecai just up and vanished. Left town or dead. Nobody knew exactly. Except Dylan, I guess.

"He's lived out here in the woods for a while now,"

Dylan says, scratching the back of his neck the way Daddy does sometimes. "I've run into him a couple of times when I'm hunting, but he usually keeps his distance."

I think about Mama and poor little Peetie Munn and wonder if the world's worst police detective has linked the two cases yet. I doubt it. Frank probably doesn't even know what a *cold case* is. If he watched more TV, he'd know that they make whole shows about them.

"Is he dangerous?" I ask.

Dylan shrugs and sits on our log pew by the fire. "He's big enough that he could be if he wanted. My daddy's told me some pretty crazy stories about Mordie. Says he ain't right in the head."

I claim the spot on Dylan's right before Gary or Carl can. Carl kneels on the ground beside Tucker, who has completely bottomed out from all the excitement, panting so hard his rib cage expands and deflates like a giant furry accordion.

Dylan shakes his head like we're just a bunch of dumb little kids who don't do what they're told. "I guess I can hang out here until morning, but then y'all need to head back to the tree line."

"I can't go back," I say, my voice way whinier than I'd intended.

When Dylan turns to me, I realize how close I sat down next to him. His face is so near to mine that his nicotine-scented breath tickles my nose. As nasty as cigarette breath usually is, coming out of Dylan's mouth it has a totally different effect on me. Like magic fairy dust that makes me dizzy and tingly all over.

I look him straight in the eyes and keep my voice steady. "I have to find the Whispers. They know where my mama is."

Dylan holds my gaze a moment, the reflection of the fire dancing in his sad, rust-colored eyes. He glances over at Gary, who just shrugs in response. Dylan looks down and sighs like a weary old man. He lifts his cap off his head, wipes his brow with the back of his hand, and then recrowns himself—King of the Redneck Superheroes. It's a very grown-up-looking thing to do, like Dylan is a full-on adult man trapped inside the body of a fourteen-year-old boy. That is, a fourteen-year-old boy who kicked puberty's butt way earlier than most kids his age.

We all watch him. Even Tucker lies there staring up at him, as if waiting for his orders. Dylan has that way about him—he's in charge now and we're helpless to make a decision without him. He sighs again, loud and sounding annoyed that we screwed up his plans, whatever those were. Skipping town, from the looks of it.

"Just get some sleep," he finally says, looking at us. "I'll stay up and keep watch in case Mordie comes back."

I exhale, feeling instantly safer and less like I want to run all the way home hollering at the top of my lungs like a Pentecostal preacher at a tent revival. But the idea of falling asleep and peeing myself with just Gary and Carl around was bad enough. No way can that happen now that Dylan is staying.

"I'm not very sleepy," I lie. "I can stay up and help you keep watch."

"Cool," Dylan says, but I can't tell if he really cares or if he's just humoring me.

Humoring someone doesn't have anything to do with telling jokes. It's more like saying whatever you think someone wants to hear just so they'll shut the heck up.

Like, *I don't care if Dylan is just humoring me or not, because I think sitting by the fire with him all night is a winsome idea.*

Gary stokes the fire with a stick the length of his arm. "I don't think we're going to get much sleep tonight. We all might as well just stay up."

Traitor.

"I want to go home," Carl whines. I knew that was coming. *Strike three.*

"Shut it, Carl," I say. I give him a hard look, silently scolding him to man up. It's a look I know well because I've gotten it from Daddy a lot over the past few months.

Dylan slides his tightly Levi'd butt down off the log pew onto the ground beside Tucker, who sidles up next to him. He rests his arm on Tucker's back and runs his fingers through the thick fur. They look like they belong together. I don't know which one I'm more jealous of—Dylan for stealing the attention of my dog, or Tucker for having actual physical contact with Dylan Mathews, King of the Redneck Superheroes. His hands are probably rough from working the farm all day, but I don't guess I'd mind too much if he wanted to scratch my neck too—not that he would ever want to. I know I'm nowhere near as beautiful as Dylan, but I've been told I'm very sweet. Like *a lot.*

Danny walks up holding a video game in his hand. "Mama, can I get this?"

I glance over at the game. There're some real muscular army guys on the cover, so I hope she says yes. Mama looks at the price tag and her forehead crinkles.

"That one's too expensive, sweetie," she says to Danny. "Go try to find something cheaper. A lot cheaper."

Danny rolls his eyes and huffs. "Dang, Mama." He stalks away.

Mama calls after him, "Watch that mouth, young man, and don't be so melodramatic. It's just a game."

I grab the family-size pack of Walmart brand toilet paper we usually get and drop it into our cart.

"Thanks, Button," Mama says, studying her shopping list.

"Mama?" I say.

She marks toilet paper off her list. "Hmmm?"

"What does melodramatic *mean?"*

She looks at me and smiles, then touches her chin with the cap of the ink pen for a second before answering. "Melodramatic is like when you show your tail over something that really doesn't amount to a hill of beans."

I giggle thinking about Mama calling Danny melodramatic. And that she said tail.

She pushes our cart forward and winks at me. "Use it in a sentence, Button."

I squint my left eye and twist my mouth, which sometimes helps me think of good sentences when we're playing the word-of-the-day game.

"Grandma had a very melodramatic reaction when Mr. Killen stopped carrying Birds Eye Deluxe Halved Strawberries (in syrup)."

Mama laughs out loud, like she doesn't care if all of Walmart hears her. "She sure did. Good one, Button."

"Carolyn?" a female voice calls out. "Carolyn James?"

Mama and I both look up to find a dark-headed woman smiling at us and holding a plastic shopping basket. She's rail thin and just okay looking—not beauty-queen pretty like Mama, but that's not the woman's fault, so who am I to judge?

"Sandy?" Mama says, sounding surprised. They walk to each other and hug.

"I didn't know you were in town," Mama says, holding the woman at arm's length. "What's it been, two years?"

"I know," the woman says. "Too long. And Mother is not about to let me hear the end of it, believe you me. Just here for a quick visit."

Before Miss Sandy notices me, Danny pops up out of nowhere and shoves a different game in Mama's face—no muscular army men on the cover this time. I checked.

"Can we afford this one, Mama?" he says, being rude as usual.

Mama pushes the game down out of her face and smiles at Miss Sandy.

"Oh my God!" Miss Sandy says. "Is this Danny?"

Mama nods and Danny smiles that big toothpaste-commercial smile of his at her. He only pulls it out when he knows grown-ups are about to tell him how good-looking he is. I creep up behind Mama, hoping to get a similar reaction.

"He was always THE most beautiful child," Miss Sandy says to Mama. "Remember how everyone thought he was a girl when he was little?" They both laugh, Miss Sandy way more than Mama. Danny rolls his eyes. He's heard this a thousand times before and he never likes it.

"And now he is THE most handsome young man," Miss Sandy says. "You and Daniel must be so proud."

I lean against Mama's backside, a little worried now about being compared to Danny and all of his beauty-ness and handsome-ness. But Mama's not having it, because I feel her whole body stiffen. She never likes one of us to be left out in favor of the other. She steps aside and pushes me forward, right in front of Miss Sandy.

"Thank you," Mama says. "And you remember Riley, don't you?"

Miss Sandy gives me that oh-bless-your-heart head cock and tight smile, like she's constipated or something.

"Of course I do," she says, slapping her palms on her thighs like she's totally lying. Or like she thinks I'm a stray puppy. "Little Riley. Always THE sweetest little boy."

That's it. That's all I ever get. Sweet. She's back to fawning over Danny and running her fingers through his thick, wavy brown hair. It's okay. I'm used to it. Danny may have movie-star good looks, but he's a squirrel serial killer and I'm not.

"Well, it's so good to see you, hon, but I have to get a move on,"

Miss Sandy says. "Mother's waiting in the car and you know how impatient she gets."

"Tell her I asked about her," Mama says, even though she didn't ask about Miss Sandy's impatient mother. They hug again. Before Miss Sandy walks away, she gives Danny a kiss on the cheek, leaving a smudge of red lipstick, and then musses my hair. I hate it when people muss my hair. It's like a lame consolation prize.

A consolation prize *is a crappy parting gift they give losers on game shows that's nowhere near as good as the grand prize—sort of like a participation ribbon.*

As in, When I was born, Mama and Daddy must have thought I was a consolation prize baby because you can't win the grand prize twice in a row.

Mama pulls me close to her side and squeezes my shoulder. "Danny, go put that back. It's still too expensive."

Danny huffs and puffs as he walks away but doesn't talk back. I watch him until he turns the corner.

"Will I always be the ugly, sweet one?" I don't know why I said it out loud. I was just thinking it and the words just kind of jumped out of my mouth. Some words have a mind of their own.

Mama looks down at me. "Hey."

"Hey," I say back, looking up at her.

She winks at me. "Why do I call you Button?"

I roll my eyes, but can't stop my lips from curling up. " 'Cause you think I'm cute as a button."

She nods. "That's right. And whoever heard of such a thing as an ugly button?"

I giggle.

"I mean, what would happen if there were no buttons in the world?" she says, her eyes all big and crazy-looking.

"We have to have buttons, Mama," I say, still giggling. "Or else our shirts and pants would fall off."

She starts pushing our cart down the aisle again and nods once. "That's right, sweetie. The world would be one hot mess without buttons."

16

THE MOST PERFECT MOMENT IN THE HISTORY OF MOMENTS

Gary has finally calmed Carl down by playing the superhero game as they lie on top of their sleeping bags next to the fire. They're wolfing down some of Mr. Killen's World Famous Boiled Peanuts and tossing their empty shells into a brown paper bag like they're shooting hoops.

I look over at Dylan. He stares into the fire as he spoils Tucker with the longest neck scratch in the history of neck scratches. Tucker's eyelids droop with pleasure like he's high on the devil's weed or something. Feeling the need to reclaim Tucker's attention, I slide down off the log pew and join Dylan on the ground. Tucker immediately pops up, circles the fire, and lands right next to me, like I knew he would. He gives me an apology lick on the side of the face and then settles on my left. I forgive him and rest my arm on his back, digging my fingers down into the soft, thick fur of his neck.

"Wow," Dylan says, grinning through a yawn. "I guess he knows who's the boss."

I shrug like it's no big deal. "I'm the one who feeds him every day."

Dylan chuckles a little. "Yeah, I can't compete with that."

We sit there in silence—leaning against the log pew, staring into the flames, our shoulders only inches apart. The fire crackles, pops, and hisses like it's telling us a story. Nature's symphony blends into the background of the shadowy woods around us like a movie soundtrack, rising and falling in volume in all the right places. If Gary and Carl weren't on the other side of the fire arguing about a possible Deadpool and Spider-Man matchup, I might even call it romantic.

Romantic is when you're with someone you like a lot and you're having a moment so special that all the butterflies racing around in your stomach make you want to vomit.

Like, *It wouldn't be very romantic if I vomited on Dylan right now.*

"So, you really think the Whispers know where your mama is?" Dylan asks, looking at me with one eyebrow raised. I can't tell if it's raised because he also hopes the Whispers know where she is or because he thinks I'm crazy for believing it.

I count the freckles on his nose for like the hundredth time. *Still seven.* Nodding, I turn my attention back to the fire so there's a normal reason for the heat in my cheeks.

"Yeah," I say. "You probably think that's dumb."

"Nah. I understand a thing or two about missing your mama."

I don't know what to say. I've never seen a woman around the Mathews farm. Just Dylan and his mean-as-asnake-looking daddy. But I don't remember ever hearing tell of his mother dying or anything. I want to ask, but it feels too personal. He throws a pinecone on the fire. Like a period. End of story. Next subject. So I drop it.

When I turn a little to face him, my knee falls onto his. He doesn't pull away or seem freaked out or anything, so I leave it there. My heart thumps hard in my chest. I pray it stays quiet and doesn't try to send Dylan some kind of Morse code warning message about *my other condition.*

"Do you think Mordecai hurt that boy that went missing?" I ask, hoping Dylan won't notice that our knees are touching and beat the crap out of me.

Dylan looks over at me and does that thing again where he lifts the bill of his cap, wipes his forehead with the back of his hand, and then lowers the cap.

"Heck if I know," he says. "But whatever happened to Peetie Munn, people around here sure blame Mordie." He stares straight ahead, the firelight flickering across his blank face. "I wouldn't put it past him, though."

"Is that why you held your gun on him?" I ask. "Did you think he was going to hurt us?"

He shrugs and looks away. "I've heard a lot of stories about him over the years. None of them good. My daddy says when they were little, Mordie had a thing for torturing and killing small animals for sport. Hid their carcasses under the house."

I gag a little imagining the smell. I also wonder if Danny will grow up to be a hobgoblin and live alone in the woods because he likes killing innocent squirrels for sport. Seems likely.

"He used to drink a lot, too," Dylan adds. "They say the whiskey brought out Mordie's dark side. Heard he nearly killed a guy in a bar fight one time."

I want to ask Dylan if he thinks Mordecai Mathews could have taken my mother, but I guess I should be careful about revealing my suspicions to a member of Mordecai's family. Mama always says *blood is thicker than water*.

"What does your daddy think of Mordie now?" It's all I can think to say, but it makes Dylan's face go dark.

"My daddy ain't no count neither," he says. "All the Mathews men got something rotten inside them."

Dylan stares into the fire, his eyes glassy. I don't even think he realizes it, but he touches the bruise on his face. A single tear scurries out the corner of his eye and runs down his cheek. That's when I know. His daddy did that to his face. That's why he has all those clothes in his backpack. He's running away from home. I also know that even though my daddy doesn't love me anymore, he would never do that to me, or to Danny.

Dylan wipes the tear away with the back of his balled fist and clears his throat. I can't tell if he's embarrassed or not, though. He just picks up another pinecone and throws it on the fire. Another period. End of story.

I look away to give him a moment of privacy and realize that Gary and Carl have gone silent. They're both asleep on top of their sleeping bags. Gary snorts a little as he rolls over, turning away from us. It's just Dylan and me surrounded by the soothing chords of nature's symphony. It feels like we're the only two people in the world and we're getting our own private concert. I don't dare move my knee away from Dylan's. He doesn't move his away either. It's like there's an electric current running back and forth between us through the small spot where our knees touch. It's exciting and dangerous all at the same time. It's also the most perfect moment in the history of moments.

I rest my head against the log pew and close my eyes, listening to the evening song around us. The cicadas have a solo right now. When they're done, the frogs bring in the bass line. Then come the birds and the crickets joining in on the chorus. I don't know if it's how comfortable I am, or the touch of Dylan's knee, or the natural music of the woods, but the song Mama wrote for me nearly breaks through the fog in my brain. But it slips away again before I can hear it in my head. I don't even realize I've fallen asleep until I'm awakened by a warm, wet trickle running down my leg.

I panic. Scramble to my feet and can only stop the flow for about five or six steps into the cover of darkness. With my back to the campsite, I unzip, pull it out, and release the pressure just in the nick of time. The stream of pee is strong and noisy as it hits the fallen leaves. The sound reminds me of the rain beating down on the tin roof of Daddy's work shed, which unfortunately reminds me of Kenny from Kentucky. Another wave of guilt washes over me.

Riley James, how do you plead?

Guilty, your honor.

I shake the memory loose and tuck it back where it belongs—behind the big wall in my brain where I put things I don't want to think about too much.

When the pee flow finally stops, I look down and check my pants. Luckily there's only a small dark spot, not much more than you get when you don't shake enough at the toilet before putting your thing away. The pee didn't get close to the Ziploc bag in my pocket. Mama's ring is safe once again. I don't dare look over my shoulder for fear that Dylan is watching me. But when I'm finally finished and everything is back where it belongs, I slowly turn around. The first thing I notice is that Dylan is asleep just like Gary and Carl. The secret of *my condition* is still safe and I finally exhale for the first time since I woke up. The second thing I notice sends another jolt of panic through my body.

Tucker is gone.

I hurry over to my backpack, fish out the flashlight, and click it on. It flickers a moment and then casts a dim but steady beam of light into the darkness surrounding our camp. I point the light straight ahead—then to my left and my right. Nothing but trees. I'm about to wake Dylan when Tucker's whine calls to me from somewhere out in the darkness. It's that high-pitched whine he makes when he's worried about something and can't explain to me what it is. He's been doing it a lot since Mama disappeared. It doesn't sound like he's too far away.

I glance over my shoulder. Gary and Carl haven't moved.

Dylan's head rests against the log pew and a soft purr barely parts his swollen lips. I decide not to wake them. After all, Tucker probably just went to do his business like I did. But it's dark and the last thing I want to do is get lost out here looking for him. I ease over to the fire as quietly as I can and pick up Gary's bag of empty peanut shells.

Tucker's distant whine calls out to me again and I follow it, clutching the flashlight in one hand and the remains of Mr. Killen's World Famous Boiled Peanuts in the other. I stick close to the creek, trying to keep my steps light and quiet, which sounds way easier than it really is. Leaves crunch and branches snap angrily underfoot, like they're irritated that I woke them from a peaceful sleep. The beam of my flashlight dims. I shake it and the light brightens a bit.

I stop walking and allow the noisy ground cover to quiet down around my feet so I can get my bearings. Tucker's call echoes ahead, bouncing from one tree to another. It sounds like it's coming from the left. But to follow it would mean crossing the creek into straight-up hobgoblin territory. Land of Mordecai Mathews and who knows what else. Maybe the land of the Whispers. I glance over my shoulder. The light of the campfire is a small bright spot of safety behind me, though its glow is shrinking and the outlines of my sleeping friends and my own personal redneck superhero have blurred.

I take a few steps more, casting the beam of the flashlight over the creek until I spot the narrowest and shallowest point I can find. Part of a log even bridges most of the way across. This could have been where Tucker crossed over.

I put the weight of one foot on it, testing its sturdiness, satisfied that I could balance on it half the way and jump the rest if it gives out under me.

Peering into the utter darkness on the other side of the creek, I call in a forced whisper, hoping not to wake any sleeping hobgoblins, "Tucker."

He whines again in response. But I don't hear his footsteps, which is strange because he always comes when I call. Something's wrong. I take a deep breath of crisp night air, the familiar scent of honeysuckle and jasmine calming me. With my dog urging me forward and the safety of the campsite, Dylan, and Dylan's shotgun behind me, I step onto the log and cross over to the other side.

17

THE SMARTEST DOG IN THE HISTORY OF DOGS

I don't know how long I've been walking, but I'm nearly out of boiled peanut shells. I've been dropping a couple every few feet, feeling pretty smart for thinking to use them as markers so I don't get lost out here in the land of Mordecai Mathews. I guess I could've used Funyuns, but then my path probably would've been eaten up by squirrels or deer. I know Funyuns are just as delicious to animal persons as they are to human persons because Tucker loves them, even though they give him major gas.

I try not to think about how dark it is just beyond the beam of my flashlight and I don't dare look to my right or my left. There could be a hobgoblin walking right beside me and I wouldn't even know. Don't want to know. Tucker's call has been steady, like he knows I'm coming and he's guiding me toward him with some kind of canine GPS. Tucker would have made a great police dog. Or maybe he could play one on TV. They could make a whole show about him. But I know Tucker would never leave me for the glitz and glamour of Hollywood.

A branch snaps up ahead and I freeze.

"Tucker?"

He whines again. Somewhere over to my right. I change course and go in that direction, trying not to think about the fact that the sound I just heard was straight ahead and not to my right. *Just a deer,* I think, trying to convince myself.

My last few boiled peanut shells later, I hear his heavy panting ahead. When I spot his outline, bathed in an open stream of moonlight, I'm so relieved I could cry. I drop the empty bag and run the rest of the way to him. Tucker sits there in the center of a wide circle of moonlight, like an alien spaceship is about to beam him aboard. I look up, just to make sure. No spaceship. I want to hug him, but now that I know he's okay and not about to be abducted by aliens, all I can think about is how angry I am at him.

I plant my hands on my hips like I do when I scold him, which isn't very often. "Why'd you run off?"

My tone is as harsh as I can make it. He doesn't answer me. He never does. But that's never stopped me from asking him questions before.

"You trying to get us both lost out here? Or eaten alive? Or abducted by aliens?" He closes his mouth and cocks his head at me, like he doesn't understand why I'm so mad at him. That's when I notice that nature's symphony has gone completely silent. It must be intermission. I glance around, making sure that we're alone, the getting-eaten-alive part of my own words haunting me now. And that's when I see it. That's when I understand. That's when I almost pee myself again with excitement because Tucker is hands-down the smartest dog in the history of dogs.

I turn slowly and look around just to make sure this isn't a dream. I'm standing in the middle of a clearing about as big as my bedroom, nothing on the ground but a carpet of crunchy dead leaves. I gaze up. There's an opening in the treetops like a gaping hole in the ceiling of the woods. The moon shines down on us, making the whole area glow like an oasis in the middle of the forest.

An *oasis* is a place in the desert with water and palm trees where you can lay out, drink coconut milk, and forget for a few minutes that you're still stranded out in the middle of the desert.

Tucker walks his front paws forward and slides the rest of the way down onto his belly in slow motion. And there it is. Sitting right behind him in the dead center of the clearing—a rotted-out tree stump about as high as my waist. Just like in the story of the Whispers. I try to move toward it but my legs are like jelly. I drop the flashlight. A small gust of wind swirls around my body, like it's trying to help me move forward. I finally take an unsteady step around Tucker and walk over to the stump. It's about as big around as a dinner plate and hollowed out a few inches deep, kind of like a huge wooden cereal bowl. I run my fingers around the rim, the dry dead bark snagging my skin.

A familiar scent tickles my nose and I look up to find honeysuckle bushes surrounding the clearing. The scent is strong and I can almost taste the sweet nectar of their blooms on my tongue. Something buzzes my right ear and I duck. A flicker like tiny blue Christmas lights flashes in the corner of my eye, but when I snap my head around in that direction, it's gone. Tucker watches me, his eyes wide and his head still cocked. That's his *my human is a nut job* look. I get that a lot from him.

"You found it, Tuck," I say, unable to stop a wide grin from stretching out my face. "Good boy." I reach down and scratch the top of his head. He responds with a solid tail whack to the ground.

I stare down into the stump like I'm waiting for some kind of secret door to open up in there. I imagine my body shrinking in size. Falling down the hole and landing in some kind of Whispers Wonderland where I find Mama sitting around eating cake and ice cream with a crazy-looking dude in a big top hat. *If only.*

Riley.

Just like last time, their voices are both right in my ear and also, somehow, everywhere—sailing through the treetops on a rippling magic carpet of wind, leaves, and the smell of honeysuckle. The blue Christmas lights fade in and out around me, but they're so quick I can't be sure if I'm just seeing spots, like when you close your eyes real tight. I try not to look directly at them so I won't have to stay here with them forever like in the story, but I know they're here. And I won't waste this chance.

I slip my hand down into my pocket slowly, like any sudden movement might scare them away or wake me up from this dream that I don't want to wake up from. I ease the Swiss Army knife out of my pocket and cup it in my hand. Holding it over the stump, I look up into the trees. I don't know if that's where they're watching me from, but it feels like the right place to look.

"I brought this for you," I say, my voice raised enough to be clearly heard but not come off as disrespectful. "It's my grandpa's. He's going to be real mad that I took it, but I don't care. I want you to have it. It's a tribute."

No answer. Just my whispered name again.

"Do you know where my mama is?" I ask with a slight crack in my voice. "I need to find her. I think she might be in trouble."

Another gust of warm honeysuckle wind covers me like a sweet-smelling blanket fresh out of the dryer. I know they can hear me. They understand. The wind dies down. Tucker rises up into a sitting position and watches me. The look in his eyes tells me that he would give anything if he could speak my language right now so he could help me. But I understand his stare just fine. He thinks I'm doing this wrong.

I place Grandpa's Swiss Army knife inside the tree stump and take a step back. I pause and consider my words carefully. "It's my heart's desire to find Mama."

A few moments pass. The wind dies down. The tiny voices grow silent, and no flickering blue Christmas lights tease the corners of my eyes. I have one of those moments where I think I imagined it all—the Whispers, the hobgoblin, Redneck Superhero Dylan Mathews showing up and saving us. Maybe it's all been a dream. Maybe any minute now I'll wake up in my pee-soaked bed.

No. It has to be real. Because if it isn't, that means—

Another branch snaps in the darkness, just beyond the clearing, and I jerk my head around. I stare in that direction, waiting for Mama to step forward. I can't believe it was that easy. I can't believe I doubted them. The Whispers *are* real. They've given me my heart's desire. Now I watch the dark doors of the forest, wondering which one she's about to step through.

Tucker pushes up off the ground, the hair on his spine rising—never a good sign. He backs up and growls—his threatening growl, not his playful one. I reach down, pick up the flashlight, and point it into the darkness straight ahead. The shadowy figure that steps forward, about to cross the border of the moonlit ground, is *not* Mama. It's too big to be Mama. Too tall. Too wide. Too hairy. Too . . . *hobgobliny*.

A high-pitched scream sails out of my mouth before I can stop it. It pierces the night sky, stopping the hobgoblin in his tracks. Actually the thing takes a step back. Like *I* scared *it*. Tucker growls and crouches like he's going to attack. But I'm afraid even Tucker wouldn't have a chance against a hobgoblin.

Yanking on his collar, I pull him in the opposite direction. I stumble back but quickly regain my footing. With the flashlight gripped firmly in my other hand, I back out of the clearing. I turn and scour the ground for empty boiled peanut shells. The shaky beam of light finally lands on the empty bag, and then two shells, then three. I follow their path, Tucker and I both running. Trying not to trip and fall. I don't look back because I don't want to know if the hobgoblin is chasing us. Surely he'd have caught us by now. My heart pounds away in my chest, like it's trying to call 911 in Morse code. I hope it gets through to Frank. I'd take the world's worst police detective over anybody right about now.

The peanut shells lead us in the direction of safety, and the farther away from the clearing we get, the easier it is to run. I don't know if that was Mordecai Mathews back there or one of his hobgoblin buddies, but I don't slow down to find out. I keep one hand firmly on the flashlight and the other on Tucker's collar so he's not tempted to run back and attack the hobgoblin. Tucker can hold his own with any human or animal person, but this is something else entirely. Something dark. Something evil. Something that eats little boys named Peetie Munn and steals sleeping mothers right out of their living room.

I just run.

18

THE F-WORD

We made it back. Tucker goes straight over to the creek bank and starts lapping up water while I plop down onto the log pew, hanging my head between my legs to catch my breath. The early-morning twilight bathes our campsite in an eerie haze. Gary, Carl, and Dylan are just waking up and I don't think they even realize that I've been gone. When I look up, the three of them are standing in front of me—all wrinkled faces, cocked heads, and squinty eyes full of sleep and questions.

Through my panting, I tell them about Tucker running off in the middle of the night. About the boiled peanut shells. And the clearing. And hearing my name and the glowing blue lights. And about leaving Grandpa's Swiss Army knife in the rotted-out tree stump as a tribute for the Whispers. I don't realize how fast I'm talking and how crazy my story probably sounds until I stop to take a deep breath.

They don't believe me.

I know because they all stare at me like I'm some kind of wack-job who needs a straitjacket.

A *straitjacket* isn't something you wear because you're cold. It's something they put on you to hold your arms down when you're sick in the head, raving like a lunatic, and foaming at the mouth.

As in, *I wipe my mouth with the back of my hand and thankfully there isn't any foam there, so I don't need a straitjacket just yet.*

I decide it's best to end my story there, leaving out the second sighting of the hobgoblin. If I didn't, they might never have agreed to go back to the clearing with me to investigate.

When the sun wakes up completely, and after a quick breakfast of Vienna sausages, Funyuns, and warm Mountain Dew, we cross the creek at the same place I did a few hours earlier. We follow the path I marked with the empty shells of Mr. Killen's World Famous Boiled Peanuts. Dylan leads the way, his shotgun resting on his shoulder like he was born with it there. I follow behind him, staring at his V-shaped back, his wide shoulders, and the way his jeans hang low on his narrow hips. Silently, I ask God to forgive me for staring at Dylan like that. That's what the preacher at the North Creek Church of God says we should do when we have unclean thoughts. It's confusing because the thoughts caused by *my other condition* never feel unclean in my heart, but my brain knows better. My brain has learned more about the world from church and school than my heart has.

I guess it makes sense that brains are smarter than hearts. Because of them being . . . well, brains.

Gary and Carl are behind me, arguing as usual. Carl is still rattled by the first Mordecai Mathews sighting last night and wants to go home. I wish he would.

Tucker pulls up the rear. He's slow and panting a lot this morning. He wouldn't eat the kibble I packed for him until I stood over him and made him eat it. I could tell by the way he looked up at me between bites that he only finished it because he didn't want to disobey me. But that's the only way I can get him to eat these days. Maybe Tucker just dreads going back into the land of Mordecai Mathews this morning. That I understand. But I feel pretty safe walking behind Dylan, his shoulders, and his shotgun.

I don't know how long we walk, but my feet hurt and my lungs feel like they're full of rocks instead of air. You'd think Gary would be dying with the extra weight he carries around, but he's always had a lot of energy for a jumbo-size kid.

Even with all the noise of our feet plowing through crunchy leaves and brittle branches, the name rings in my ears like that eyeball-rattling fire alarm at school. I think Carl says it. *Kenny.* As in Kenny from Kentucky. My face heats from the inside out, but I don't dare look back at him. I just keep my mouth shut, my eyes forward, and listen.

"Mama said Aunt Sadie is coming to visit next month and Kenny's coming with her," Carl says.

"Dang it!" Gary says. "I hate that dude."

"He's nice to me," Carl says.

"That's because you're a little kid. Everyone's nice to little kids."

"You're not," Carl shoots back.

Gary doesn't respond to that and I can barely breathe. Kenny from Kentucky is coming. Next month.

"He's not staying in my room again," Gary says to Carl, but loud enough so all creation can hear him. "He can sleep in your room or on the couch."

I can't believe they're talking about Kenny from Kentucky, and in front of Dylan.

"Who's Kenny?" Dylan asks.

I glance up and see that he's looking over his shoulder at me. Why would Dylan ask me who Kenny is? I'm not the one talking about him. I shrug and act like I've never heard the name before. Finally Gary chimes in.

"He's our aunt Sadie's new stepson," Gary says. "She moved to Kentucky when she married Kenny's dad. He's Mexican."

"You got a problem with Mexicans?" Dylan asks. I act like I'm invisible. I want no part of this conversation. *None.*

"I don't give a crap that he's Mexican, but that kid can be a real pain sometimes," Gary says. "Acts like he's better than all of us put together. His dad's rich or something, and Kenny dresses all fancy."

Dylan chuckles as he kicks some brush out of our path.

For some reason it feels like he's laughing at me as much as Kenny from Kentucky. "Fancy how?"

Gary says, "You know, always telling you which stores his clothes came from and how expensive they were. He's a real priss pot that way."

Priss pot? *That way*? Heat floods my cheeks.

Gary adds, "And he acts like we're a bunch of dumb country hicks."

"Sounds like he doesn't like his visits here any more than you do," Dylan says.

"Oh, he hates coming to our house," Gary says, because he will *not* shut up about Kenny for some reason. "Likes to remind us how much smaller our house is compared to his. Dude's just flat-out rude. We're the same age, so our parents think we should be like instant best friends or something. Last time they came to visit, Kenny spent more time with Riley than he did with us, and that was just fine by me. He liked your daddy's work shed, didn't he, dawg?"

A wave of nausea hits me hard and fast. My ears feel like they are on fire. My heart's beating so hard it's about to have a heart attack.

I turn around, glare at Gary, and fail to keep my voice down to normal *strolling through the woods with friends* levels. "Why don't you just shut your big mouth, fatso?"

I holler it, actually, and my voice echoes through the trees. Everyone stops walking—even Tucker, who cocks his head and gives me his *what the heck, dude?* look. Gary stares at me with his eyes wide and his mouth hanging open. I'm as shocked as he looks. I've never told him to shut up before, and I've *never* called Gary the F-word. I've never even so much as told him he might need to eat more salads and less Funyuns. I lower my gaze and turn forward again.

Dylan stands there looking at me with both eyebrows raised up to Jesus. "You okay? Your face is all red."

"I'm fine!" I don't really say it as much as I bark it and my face heats up even more. How dare I speak to the King of the Redneck Superheroes in that tone?

I look at my feet, and the leaves, and the dirt, and anything other than Dylan's eyes, bruised jaw, and swollen lip.

When I glance up, he's still staring at me. I feel like a real butthole for yelling at him. I wonder if this is how Danny feels all the time. Or how Frank feels when he can't solve a case. I try to stuff my shame and anger down deep inside me, but it refuses to go away quietly. I have the uncontrollable need to blame this all on Gary.

"He just keeps running his fat mouth so much, he's probably scaring the Whispers away." There I go again with the F-word. What the heck is wrong with me? It's like the devil has taken over my soul. Maybe he has.

I look back at Gary. I can hardly bear to meet his gaze. When I finally do, I see it's glassy and his cheeks are red as fire. He looks at me a long time, the hurt in his eyes clear as a bell.

"There's no such thing as the Whispers," Gary says with a hard edge in his voice, drilling a hole in me with his eyes and his words. He's trying to hurt me back and I deserve it. But he's gone too far. The Whispers are my only hope of finding Mama. Gary knows that. To say they're not real is like saying I'll never find her.

"We're just going along with this to make you feel better," he says.

Dylan, Carl, and Tucker are watching us. I'm so mad I can't even respond.

"Nobody believes you," Gary says. "Not even Dylan."

That knocks the air right out my lungs. My eyes sting with unexpected tears, but I fight to hold them back. I feel Dylan looming behind me, but he doesn't say anything. He doesn't call Gary a big fat liar or tell him to shut up. And without Tucker by my side, I feel completely alone.

Gary turns abruptly and heads back in the direction we came. "Come on, Carl. We're going home."

Carl follows him without a second look at me. Tucker sits there staring up at me and panting, waiting for my next move. I can't bring myself to look at Dylan and have him confirm what Gary just said. A moment longer than forever passes before he says anything.

"We should probably go back with them so they don't get lost," Dylan finally says behind me. "I've got to head out pretty soon anyway."

I finally turn to meet his eyes, but they give nothing away. They don't deny what Gary said, but they don't confirm it either. He just looks at me with his swollen lip, bruised jaw, and seven nose freckles. Then he moves past me and follows Gary and Carl. And I guess that's my answer. Nobody believes me. Especially not the King of the Redneck Superheroes.

Tucker takes a couple of steps and for a second I think he's going to leave me too. But he just goes over to a tree and throws up his breakfast in three violent heaves.

He looks like I feel.

19

KENNY FROM KENTUCKY

I don't follow them. I stand there watching them disappear into the thick cover of the woods. They don't look back either. It's like they don't even care if I'm following them or not. As least Tucker hasn't abandoned me. When he's done throwing up, he sits there staring at me, probably wondering what the plan is now. But heck if I know. Who does he think I am? Detective Chase Cooper or something?

I can't even think straight. I'm so mad at Gary, and at the same time, I feel terrible for calling him the F-word the way I did. *Twice!* But Gary really hit a nerve with all that Kenny talk.

Mama says *hitting a nerve* is not a medical term like it sounds. Well, I guess it could be. Like if the world's worst doctor is operating on you and cuts right into a nerve by mistake. Like if Frank left the police force and became a doctor, he'd probably do something like that. But it's also when someone says something that makes you real mad because it's at least part of the way true and a little embarrassing.

As in, *What Gary said about Kenny from Kentucky really hit a nerve because it was all the way true and a lot embarrassing.*

Kenny did like my daddy's work shed, but not because he was interested in all the tools Daddy keeps in there. He liked it because it was private, especially during the day when Daddy was at work. I don't think Daddy liked Kenny very much. *That boy's got a little sugar in his tank,* he said once, and I don't think he was talking about the watermelon bubble gum Kenny chewed all the time.

I guess Gary was right about Kenny being a real priss pot too, but that didn't bother me about him. I thought he was funny and interesting—*so* different from Gary, Carl, and the other kids at school. I liked the way he looked, too. The color of his light brown skin. The way his thick, dark hair sat politely in frozen waves on his head. The way his clothes were always spotless and neatly pressed. The way his big round eyes seemed to gobble up everything in sight, including me. And the way his lips were so red, almost like he put lipstick on them, but I don't think he did. It was probably from all the watermelon bubble gum, which also made him smell delicious—like a big human lollipop that I wanted to lick real bad.

The week Kenny came to visit Gary's family last summer, he acted like he'd rather spend time with me than his new country stepcousins. That made me feel good. It was nice, having someone new to play with for a change—someone who knew different stuff than what they teach us in Buckingham schools. Someone who knew words in a whole other language. Someone who talked about more than just Rebecca Johnson's butt and boobs. Someone who wasn't a known squirrel murderer. And someone who wasn't afraid to admit how handsome Detective Chase Cooper on *CID: Chicago* was. That guy's so good-looking, sometimes I dream about him and then I have to change my sheets for reasons other than *my condition.*

Kenny used to talk about how one day he was going to marry Detective Chase Cooper. Just talked about it right out in front of all creation, like he didn't even care if God heard him. I didn't know it was possible for a guy to marry another guy. Maybe that kind of thing's only allowed in Kentucky. But Kenny knew about lots of stuff like that. So I guess it shouldn't have surprised me as much as it did when Kenny kissed me in Daddy's shed.

I remember it was raining.

I like the way the rain sounds hitting the tin roof of Daddy's work shed. Like a thousand firecrackers have been set off up there. Sometimes I like to just lie on the floor of the shed during a rainstorm listening to it. But today I'm not lying down. Today I'm with Gary's new stepcousin, Kenny from Kentucky. And the hard rain has cloaked us in a storm of dangerous-feeling privacy, like we're the only two people left in the world.

Kenny stands real close to me—like a lot *closer than Gary has ever stood to me, and not just because of his belly. Kenny keeps staring into my eyes like he's trying to figure something out about me. I guess he finally does, because all of a sudden he spits out his gum—right onto the floor—and puts his whole mouth on mine, all in about two seconds flat.*

My other condition *goes into hyperdrive and I freeze. I don't know what to do, so I just close my eyes and stand there with my lips sealed together real tight. But Kenny isn't having it. He forces his tongue inside my mouth and just goes to town in there like he's cleaning a kitchen or something.*

I've never kissed anyone with my tongue before. Just the idea of it always sounded gross when Danny would tell me about him doing it with girls. But it's really not gross at all with Kenny. It's a little wet and sloppy, but his lips are real soft and he smells and tastes like watermelon. He puts his hands on my arms, which are glued to my sides. I don't touch him back because that would make me complicit.

Complicit *is when somebody is doing something wrong or illegal and you help them do it, which makes you just as guilty.*

As in, I'm not about to be complicit in this Kenny from Kentucky kissing me thing, no siree bob.

But I don't try to stop it either. If they put me on the witness stand and make me swear on the Bible, I'll have to admit that I like it. A lot. Up until the moment I open my eyes and find Mama standing in the doorway, soaking wet with a look of shock or disgust twisting her face. I can't tell which exactly. Probably both.

Days felt like weeks after that, but they eventually passed. Kenny went back to Kentucky, I went back to school, and Mama started acting different around me. She didn't say anything about what happened in the shed and I prayed every night that she never would. I thought I'd die if she did. I repented for the kiss. I guess God forgave me, but that didn't even matter if Mama treated me differently from then on.

I blame Kenny, of course. He's probably kissed lots of boys before, because he seemed to really know what he was doing. It was like when Detective Chase Cooper kisses District Attorney Amanda Ramirez in the janitor's closet at the police station on *CID: Chicago* every time they get a chance. That is until the Windy City Slasher murdered her at the end of season three.

I only ever tried to kiss boys a couple of times when I was really young and didn't know any better. I was just doing what felt natural. Like the time I tried to kiss Sister Grimes's spawn of Satan son, Gene, behind the coat cubby at Buckingham Elementary.

After that day in Daddy's work shed with Kenny from Kentucky, Mama grew more and more distant. We spent less time together, especially when she took that temp job at Upton Regional Medical Center. It wasn't very steady work. She'd be there three or four hours every day for a week and then not get called to go in again until two or three weeks later. When she *did* work, she was always tired when she got home and went right to bed. Daddy didn't like that she had to take the job at the hospital at all, but he told us it was only temporary, until things got better. I think he'd been having trouble finding construction jobs, because he was at home a lot more.

Every now and then Mama would have to work the overnight shift, so Danny and I would stay over at Grandma's house because Daddy didn't come home until morning. I'd hoped he wasn't out drinking and carousing with loose women while Mama was working so hard to keep our family afloat. Grandma and Grandpa slipped me more fives and tens than usual back then. I tried to give the money to Mama so she wouldn't have to work the temp job at the hospital anymore. She wouldn't take it even though she and Daddy worried over a stack of bills a mile high on the kitchen table and whispered about them so Danny and I wouldn't hear.

Mama and I didn't go to the Walmart on Saturdays anymore either. I guess she didn't want people to see us there blowing through all of our welfare money. I'm not sure if we were really on welfare or not, but as worried as Mama and Daddy were about everything, it wouldn't surprise me. Things got so bad, we were on the prayer list of the North Creek Church of God every Sunday for months.

I think our family's financial troubles really wore Mama down during those months, because I'd catch her crying in her bedroom by herself sometimes. When I'd ask what was wrong, she'd always dry it up real fast and smile. She couldn't even sing me the song at night anymore without tearing up and her voice cracking, so she stopped singing it altogether. I know a big part of the reason she was crying all the time was because of what she caught me doing with Kenny from Kentucky.

And now she's missing and it's all my fault. Everything has gone to hell in a handbasket since that day last summer in Daddy's work shed when Mama found out about *my other condition.*

God is punishing me. Just like Sister Grimes the Gossip said He would.

20

THE LAND OF MORDECAI MATHEWS

I have to get to the clearing and see if the Whispers accepted my tribute, so I keep going with only Tucker as backup. Apparently deer and/or squirrels find the empty shells of Mr. Killen's World Famous Boiled Peanuts just as delicious as Funyuns, because most of my path markers have disappeared. But being semi-lost out here in the land of Mordecai Mathews hasn't done much to take my mind off the return of Kenny from Kentucky. I guess I could just hide in my bedroom until he leaves. What I *should* do when Kenny gets here is march his butt right down to the police station and turn him in. Frank should be investigating him, not me. Mama was just fine until he showed up last summer.

That was also around the same time I overheard the gossip, Sister Grimes, tell someone at the church potluck that she thought I was funny. And I know she didn't mean *ha-ha* funny. She meant *funny because I want to kiss boys instead of girls* funny.

Frank should be investigating Sister Grimes, too. She

said something horrible about Mama that Sunday at the potluck. I can't remember exactly what it was, but I remember it sounded like a threat. I make a mental note to point the finger at both Kenny from Kentucky and Sister Grimes the Gossip the next time Frank hauls me down to the station for questioning.

Tucker sprints ahead of me. I pick up my pace too, and only a few steps later I'm back in the alien abduction clearing. I walk over to the tree stump. Just as I'd hoped, the Swiss Army knife is gone. A jolt of excitement charges through my body. The Whispers took it. But what happens now? When do they tell me where Mama is? I look around the clearing, half expecting her to waltz right in holding a pan of fresh-made brownies as adoring bluebirds tie yellow ribbons in her hair or something.

I scramble around the clearing looking every which-a-way and listening for the Whispers. Tucker follows me for a few minutes, but then gets tired and lies down by the tree stump with one of his *you're losing it again, dude* moans. I'm *not* losing it. I just can't figure out what I did wrong. I left the tribute, asked the Whispers to help me find Mama, they took it, but nothing happened.

The hobgoblin must have scared them away. Mordecai Mathews showed up right after I put Grandpa's Swiss Army knife inside the tree stump. He ruined my chance to find Mama. Or maybe . . .

"The Whispers were trying to tell me it was Mordecai," I say, sort of to Tucker and sort of to the tree stump. "He showed up right after I told them my heart's desire. He must have taken Mama." I look at Tucker. "We have to find him."

Tucker thumps his tail once, hard on the ground. That's always his way of telling me that he's game. He lumbers up on all fours and comes over to me, panting. Then he does something that only confirms, once again, that Tucker is hands-down the smartest dog in the history of dogs. He sniffs the left pocket of my jeans—the pocket where Mama's wedding ring rests safely in a Ziploc bag. I reach into my pocket, yank it out, and stare at it. Tucker's right. That must be why they came in my room and left it out for me to see. They want it, but they wouldn't just take it. I have to offer it as a tribute. I really don't want to give up the ring, but the Whispers can help me find the hobgoblin, and the hobgoblin has Mama. Find him, find her. And Mama's ring is the only tribute I have left. Other than my soul, that is. I think Mama would want me to try the ring first because she says my soul already belongs to Jesus.

I rip open the bag and pull out the ring even though it's not the right time of day to do this. It's not *magic time.* But it will be hours before the sun sets and Mama might not have hours. Or Mordecai Mathews could be long gone by then if he knows the Whispers ratted him out. I carefully place the ring down in the center of the rotted tree stump and take a step back, letting the empty Ziploc bag fall to the ground. Closing my eyes real tight, I whisper my wish.

"Please take me to the hobgoblin. It's my heart's desire. Show me where to find Mordecai Mathews."

I'm afraid to open my eyes. I'm afraid that when I open them, nothing will happen. That Mordecai Mathews won't appear, but the ring will be gone. But what if he's standing right behind me about to eat me and I don't even know it? I feel pretty sure Tucker would warn me if I'm about to get eaten by a hobgoblin and he's quiet as a mouse. I take the gamble and open my eyes.

No hobgoblin in sight and the ring is still right there in the tree stump. But Tucker stands at the edge of the clearing where Mordecai Mathews appeared last night. He stares out into the woods with both ears hiked up to Jesus. He hears something. Maybe he hears Mama screaming for help way out there beyond what human persons can hear.

"Tucker," I say, but he doesn't look back at me. He just stares out into the woods like he's under a spell or something.

I walk over and pat him on the head, giving him permission to lead me. "Go, Tuck."

Without a glance back at me, Tucker trots off, just fast enough that I have to jog but not so fast that I can't keep up. When I trip on a branch and lose my balance, Tucker stops and peers around at me with his *keep up, you idiot* face. I do my best and soon I have no idea where we are or how long I've been following him. I wouldn't be surprised either way if you told me it had been ten minutes or ten hours. But Tucker has a renewed energy I haven't seen in him in a long time. He's focused. Sniffing the ground as he presses forward. On a mission. And he doesn't stop until he leads me right to the door of a run-down shack tucked away in a forgotten corner of the woods.

The shack is covered in honeysuckle bushes. They run up the sidewalls and hang down off the roof like they're trying to swallow the thing whole. The little house is smaller than Daddy's shed. It leans, too. I don't see how a strong wind hasn't blown it completely away. Maybe the honeysuckle bushes hold it in place.

A fire pit made of loosely stacked stones has been constructed in front of the shack, and a rusted metal folding chair sits near it. I don't want to imagine what's been cooked in that fire pit and I try not to think about the fact that it's big enough to hold a whole deer, or a small boy like Peetie Munn, or me. In my gut, I know who lives here. There's only one possibility because Tucker's nose never lies. But I try not to think about that right now because it seems like no one's home, so it's the perfect chance to look for Mama.

Tucker circles the shack, sniffing the ground and whimpering. I can't stop staring at the door. It stands open a few inches, like an invitation to take a quick peek inside. Just to make sure Mama isn't in there. I want to believe she is, and at the same time I don't.

While Tucker explores the area behind the shack, I step up to the door and stick my head through the crack.

"Mama?" I say with a small quiver of hope.

There's no answer, but it's dark inside and I can't see much. I take a couple of steps and push the door open a few more inches. It creaks just like the door to the Windy City

Slasher's run-down house where Detective Chase Cooper found DA Amanda Ramirez's body on the season finale of *CID: Chicago*.

One more step and I'll cross the threshold. The idea of doing that seems awfully stupid. If Danny and I were watching me in a scary movie right now, we'd both be screaming at me not to go inside. But the Whispers led me here to find Mama. It cost me her wedding ring. I have to check it out. I push open the door a little more and go all the way in.

I stand in the middle of the small room looking around, waiting for my eyes to adjust to the dim lighting. By the time they do, the floor creaks behind me. I spin around, ready to bolt. But a giant hairy hobgoblin blocks my path to freedom.

21

THE HOBGOBLIN'S LAIR

Mordecai Mathews ducks as he steps inside and slowly pushes the door closed behind him. Like he's giving me one last glimpse of the world I'll never see again. I can't breathe. My heart is working overtime just to keep me from passing out. I hope my heart is smart enough to know that if I pass out right now, we're both screwed.

He's even bigger up close—taller, wider, and hairier. A bushy beard that looks like it could house a small family of squirrels hides most of his face, everything but those beady gator eyes boring a hole through me. I don't know what kind of clothes I thought hobgoblins wore, but he's actually dressed kind of normal—jeans, work boots like my dad wears, and a faded denim shirt unbuttoned over a plain white T-shirt. He looks like a grizzly bear dressed up as a human person for Halloween.

Mordecai doesn't look all that surprised to find an eleven-year-old boy standing in the middle of his one-room shack. Maybe the Whispers warned him that I was coming. Maybe they're in cahoots with him. Or maybe I remind him of Peetie Munn. After looking me over for a few seconds that feel like hours, he drops a canvas satchel on the small wooden table in the center of the room. I don't know what's in the bag and I don't really want to know because it smells terrible.

I finally exhale, slowly and quietly, but I stay perfectly still. I feel like I should say something, but everything I think of seems really lame.

Well hello there, Mr. Murder . . . I mean Mathews.

Do you speak hobgoblin or English?

I just dropped by to pick up my mama—aka your hostage—and then we'll be on our way.

Are you going to eat me now or fatten me up first?

Yeah, all pretty lame.

There's scratching and sniffing on the other side of the door and then Tucker starts barking, likely wondering why he's been shut out. He's not used to being excluded. Mordecai reaches over and slams his fist on the door—*hard.* I mean, the walls shake. It quiets Tucker instantly and makes me jump a little. Tucker whimpers and sniffs at the bottom of the door. If he knew how much danger I was in right now, I know he'd bust through that door and tear the hobgoblin to shreds. But Mordecai doesn't seem too worried about Tucker. He circles the table and pulls out the one and only metal folding chair right in front of me. It's just like the ones in the cafeteria of Buckingham Middle School, but this one is dented and rusted. He points to it. I sit, too scared to disobey his silent command.

He walks over to the corner of the room and picks up a gallon jug of water. Watching me like a hawk, he unscrews the cap and gulps at least half of the water down. Some of it runs out the sides of his mouth, getting lost somewhere in his beard. Maybe it's for the squirrel family that lives in there. He screws the cap back on and momentarily turns his back to me. Now that I have a few final moments to myself before I'm eaten alive by a big hairy hobgoblin, I steal a quick glance around the room I will die in. If by some miracle of God I'm able to escape, the police will ask me to describe the hobgoblin's lair. But a miracle of God seems unlikely, seeing as how we haven't been to the North Creek Church of God in so long and God doesn't listen to my prayers anymore.

In one corner of the room sits a black wood-burning stove with patchwork tin piping venting it up through the ceiling. There's a bed pushed against the wall that looks way too small for Mordecai. It doesn't have a real headboard or anything. The mattress sits a few inches off the floor on a simple metal frame. The bed is made, which seems funny to me, like Mordecai was expecting company. I can't imagine that hobgoblins make their beds every day just for fun. On the other wall are shelves with a bunch of books, some mismatched dishes, and tidy stacks of magazines and newspapers. I didn't know that hobgoblins could read either. I wonder if they have their own special newspapers like *The Hobgoblin Gazette* or something.

Mordecai sets the water jug on the table in front of me

and points to it. I guess he wants me to drink some and I have to admit, I'm really thirsty. My throat feels like sandpaper. I don't think he's trying to poison—or season—me because he just drank from the same jug and why would he poison—or season—himself? I pull the jug to me, unscrew the cap, and stare at the rim.

I wonder if it would be rude to wipe it off with my shirt. Otherwise I'm about to get a mouthful of hobgoblin saliva germs. His DNA could mix with mine and I might slowly be transformed into a hobgoblin over time—start growing hair in weird places, develop a hunger for human flesh, and stink to high heaven. But I don't see any way around it, so I pick up the jug by the handle, close my eyes, and drink. The water is room temperature but it still tastes good. I gulp down as much as I can, but Mordecai takes it from me mid-gulp after less than a minute. Maybe it was seasoning after all and he doesn't want to overmarinate me. He probably doesn't like his food too spicy.

"You're one of Dylan's friends," he says more than asks. "What are you doing here? Where're the rest of 'em?"

It takes me a couple of seconds to register that he actually spoke words out loud. I just assumed hobgoblins were mute, though I don't know why. But his voice is deep, round, and kind of normal sounding.

I clear my throat so my own voice won't crack like it's been known to do a lot lately. "I came alone."

Okay. That probably wasn't the smartest thing to admit to a murderous hobgoblin. Let's try this again. Detective

Chase Cooper always says to humanize yourself to your captor.

Humanize means to act like a normal, nonedible human person and not like a juicy slab of roast beef when you're sitting in front of a big hungry hobgoblin.

As in, *It's really too bad that the word* humanize *kind of rhymes with* tenderize.

"My name is Riley," I say, slowly like he might have trouble understanding. "I'm looking for my mama."

He sits down on the edge of the bed a couple of feet away from me—still within grabbing reach. I look over at the closed door. It's farther away than I'd like and Tucker has grown silent on the other side.

"Why'd you think your mama'd be here?" he says.

I have to choose my words carefully. I shouldn't just come right out and accuse him or he might decide to have me for an early dinner. I can't look him in his gator eyes, so I stare down at my hands resting in a nervous ball in my lap.

"The Whispers led me here," I say, sounding shaky, like I'm ten and not eleven.

"The Whispers," he grunts, but I don't look up. I just nod.

He pauses and then adds, "My mama used to tell me that story when I was little."

I'm shocked into silence for a couple of reasons. One, that the hobgoblin was ever *little*, and two, that he had a mama who told him bedtime stories like *The Whispers*. It's hard to imagine him having parents. Heck, it's hard to think of Mordecai Mathews as a human person at all after what he did to Peetie Munn and my mama. Maybe he was a human person once, but now he's a monster. A hobgoblin.

"What's ya mama's name?" he asks.

"Carolyn," I say. "Carolyn James."

The hobgoblin sighs and then grows quiet. His face darkens as best as I can tell under all that hair.

"You know her?"

He shifts his eyes away from mine, looking real suspicious. I wish Detective Chase Cooper were here to interrogate him. Frank would be useless. Probably take one look at Mordecai and pee himself.

"Riley," he says. And I know he means Mama's last name before she married Daddy and not my first name. "Went to school with her when I's a kid."

While I didn't know this piece of information, it's not all that surprising. Buckingham is tiny. And Detective Chase Cooper says the perp usually knows the victim.

"She was always real nice to me when the other kids weren't so much," Mordecai says, staring at the stove. He's probably wondering if he has a pot big enough to fit me in. He scratches his beard. It does look like it would itch something awful under there. I just know I need to keep him talking. If he's talking, I'm breathing.

"You knew my mama in school?"

He nods without looking at me, probably because he just said that. I better not waste my next question because it could be my last. Once he knows I suspect him of foul play, he'll have to get rid of me. I just hope he doesn't pickle my body parts in mason jars for winter. The smell of pickle juice makes me gag.

"Did . . ." I start, stop, and try again. "Did you take her? Carolyn. My mama. Is she here?"

I have a hard time getting the next one out, but finally do.

"Did you hurt her?"

He jerks his head in my direction and the sudden action nearly scares the pee out of me. But he doesn't scream in my face, or beat me over the head with his hobgoblin club. I assume they all have one. He just looks at me with those gatory eyes of his. But something in them's different now with Mama's name and memory floating around the room. His eyes mist over.

"I said she was nice to me," he says, like that's his final answer. Period. End of story.

But he didn't answer my question and the anger that's been stewing in my gut the past few weeks and months comes to a quick boil because I can tell by the look in his eyes that he knows something he's not telling me. Before I can stop myself, I lean over and scream in his hairy hobgoblin face, "What did you do to her?"

I don't think I scared him too much because he just sits there staring at me. Looking at me like *I'm* the weirdo here. Like this is *my* run-down shack out in the middle of the woods and not his.

"Did you hurt Peetie Munn too?" I say, my anger making me stupidly mouthier, which it does a lot.

Mordecai takes a deep breath. His gaze grows ice cold on me, his mouth tightens, and his voice becomes a throaty growl that grows in volume with each word.

"I. Never. Hurt. Nobody." He slams his fist on the table in front of me and I jump in my chair.

He looks down, exhaling slowly, like he feels bad for yelling at me. His hands shake. His shoulders slump, making him look smaller. He actually looks more human than hobgoblin right now. He looks almost . . . scared.

"She brought me cookies at the jailhouse, your mama," he says, staring over my head. "Said she didn't believe what they were saying I did to that boy." His eyes are glassy. "She was the only person to ever visit me there. Not even my own family came."

Mordecai takes another deep breath and wipes his eyes with the back of his hand. It's a very un-hobgoblin-like thing to do. "You said the Whispers led you here? You saw them?"

I just nod, but I don't know what to think anymore. Mordecai Mathews was my only solid lead and it cost me Grandpa's Swiss Army knife and Mama's wedding ring. In a weird way, Mordecai was my only hope. And now I'm beginning to think he might not be as guilty as I thought. Of any of it—Mama or Peetie Munn or any crime at all. Maybe he's just afraid of being accused of one again. I mean, if Mama believed him, who am I to disagree?

"What'd they look like?" he asks, his voice almost a whisper.

I swallow and sit up straight. No one's ever taken me

so seriously about the Whispers and I've never described them to anyone.

"They're small," I say. "They can fly, so I guess they have wings. And they have this blue glow to them like Christmas lights. You can only get a glimpse of them for a second or two when they're glowing. I haven't looked one directly in the eye yet. They're fast. But I guess they kind of look like . . . fairies."

I stop talking so I don't sound any crazier than usual. But Mordecai doesn't look at me like I'm crazy. He just scratches his beard, or the family of squirrels living in there, and studies me with squinted eyes. At least I think they're squinted. He has really bushy eyebrows. Now that I think about it, if there were such a thing as a hobgoblin Santa, Mordecai could totally get a job playing him in the mall at Christmas.

"Little blue fairies, huh?" he asks, his eyes more curious than glassy now.

I shrug. "Sort of."

"And they talk to you?"

I nod. "I heard them plain as day. And they took my tributes, so I know they're real."

"Tributes," he says. "Like in the story." Mordecai nods at me, but slowly like an adult who you can't tell if they believe you or they're just playing along.

"I've seen 'em too," he says. "But they ain't never talked to me."

"Where?" I ask, trying to contain my excitement. "Where did you see them?"

Mordecai rests his arms on his knees and clasps his hands together like he's about to pray. "I see 'em over by the beaver dam. Sometimes it looks like hundreds of 'em out there—hundreds of little blue fairies flying around, fading in and out. Sort of beautiful . . . and magical looking."

I nod slowly. *Magical.* I know exactly what he means.

"Maybe that's where they live," I say. "At the beaver dam."

This must be why the Whispers led me to Mordecai. He knows where to find them. Maybe that's where Mama is—with the Whispers at the beaver dam. That's probably what they meant when they said, *She's here.* They meant *here* with them. Not just *here* in the woods.

"Will you take me there?" I ask as innocently as possible without whining. "I have to find Mama before it's too late."

"Too late?" Mordecai just squint-stares at me a long time, like he can't decide if he wants to help me or eat me. My heartbeat suddenly speeds up. Hopefully it's sending him a Morse code message to do the first thing and not the second.

Finally, he sighs and looks away, shaking his head. "I can take you as far as the beaver dam if you want. It's close to the north tree line."

"You will?" A burst of energy charges through my sleep-deprived body. I don't really understand what he means by *as far as* the beaver dam when that's all the way where I want to go. But it doesn't matter. I'm going to find the Whispers and Mama, and I'm not going to get eaten by a hobgoblin— at least not today.

"I reckon you need to find your mama." Mordecai stands, towering over me like a big, hairy skyscraper. "And you can't stay here, that's for sure. You can't tell anybody you was here neither."

He grabs his canvas satchel off the table and slings it over his shoulder. "You have to leave. Now."

22

CONVERSATIONS WITH
A HOBGOBLIN

I find Tucker napping by the front door of the shack when we leave. Once he sees I'm okay, he doesn't try to rip Mordecai to shreds. He looks too tired for all that business. He just kind of semi-growls at Mordecai and sniffs him cautiously. Tucker must not like what he smells, because he backs away and becomes something Tucker never is. Timid.

Timid is when you act like you ain't got no balls.

As in, *Technically, Tucker lost his balls a long time ago, but he's never acted timid until now.*

Balls or no balls, he still plants himself between Mordecai and me as we head north, away from the shack and deeper into the woods than I've ever been.

Mordecai's legs are a lot longer than mine, and Tucker has four Rottie-shepherd legs, but I keep up as best I can. With every step my body reminds me that I've been without hardly any sleep for almost a day and a half. That's a record for me, especially without a *CID: Chicago* marathon and an endless supply of Mountain Dew. I peer up at the sky. As best as I can tell it's afternoon, but I don't have any idea if it's closer to lunchtime or suppertime. My stomach wouldn't be too picky right about now. I'd be just as happy to find a bag of Flamin' Hot Funyuns lying around out here. I don't think that's very likely, but why not hope?

Mordecai hums as we walk, like hobgoblins can actually sing or something. It crosses my mind that this could all be for show and although he's acting really casual by humming and stuff, he's really leading me deeper into the woods for reasons other than finding the Whispers. He could be marching me right into the middle of a hobgoblin convention for all I know. Hopefully Tucker will find his balls again if anything like that goes down. On the other hand, Mordecai seemed like he was telling the truth when he said he never hurt anyone, even though he was yelling and slamming his fist on the table when he said it. And Mama believed him, at least he says she did. How do I know for sure? All I can do now is stay alert and keep using Detective Chase Cooper's humanizing strategy to stay alive.

"What's that song you're humming?" I ask all sweet and innocent, like a little kid.

"Billy Joel," he kind of grunts over his shoulder.

I happen to know Billy Joel is a singer and not the name of a song, because Mama *loves* Billy Joel's music. She said Daddy used to sing "Just the Way You Are" to her all the time because it was *their song*. But I don't ask Mordecai which Billy Joel song he's humming. I try something else.

"I'm sorry I thought you hurt Mama. And Peetie," I say,

my voice raised enough so Mordecai can hear me over the crunchy leaves underfoot.

He doesn't respond. Just keeps walking and humming like I'm not even here.

"You scared the crap out of us last night," I say a little louder, trying again.

Mordecai glances over his shoulder at me but doesn't say anything and doesn't stop walking or humming.

"Why'd you do that?" I say, but not in a mean way. Just like we're two regular dudes shootin' the breeze on a normal afternoon walk through the woods and not at all like a hobgoblin tenderizing his supper with a little physical exercise.

"Just wanted y'all to go home or back to the tree line," he says with another grunt over his shoulder. "Ain't safe way out here at night. Bobcats, coyotes, and such."

I give him a second or two before I ask another question. "Was that you watching me the other night at the tree line?"

He doesn't look back at me, but he nods, confirming he was the shadow monster I saw. I don't ask him why he was watching me. I want to believe him. Believe that he was just looking out for a stupid little kid getting too close to the woods in the dark.

Tucker trots off to the left, sniffs around, and then squats. Mordecai notices and stops, I guess to let me rest while Tucker goes number two. He wipes the sweat off his forehead with his shirtsleeve and pulls a bottle of water out of his satchel. He drinks the whole thing down without offering me any. I think it's kind of rude until he pulls out another one and tosses it to me. The bottle hits me in the chest and falls to the ground before it even clicks in my brain that I'm supposed to catch it. I'm not very good at sports. That's Danny's department. I pick up the bottle and nod a quick thanks to him as I drink.

"So when was the last time you saw your mama?" he asks.

I wipe my mouth with the back of my hand. "About four months ago in our living room. She was taking a nap on the sofa. Then she went missing."

He looks at me and nods a little. Tucker trots back to us, panting really hard. He eyes my water and licks his chops. Mordecai walks over to me, kneels down, and cups his big hands together, making a water bowl for Tucker. It's a very nice thing to do. I pour some water into his hand-bowl and Tucker goes to town on it.

"Do you remember anything else about that day?" Mordecai asks.

I shrug and pour the last bit of water into Mordecai's hand-bowl for Tucker. "Not too much. I was playing outside with Gary and Carl. And there were two suspicious-looking dudes sitting in a big, fancy white car in the driveway. That's about it."

Tucker finishes all the water and then does something semi-traitorous. He licks Mordecai once on the side of the head. Then Mordecai scratches Tucker's neck. I think he even smiles at Tucker. I can't be sure under that bushy beard, but it's really hard for anyone to look at Tucker and not smile—even a possibly falsely accused hobgoblin.

"Two guys in a fancy white car, huh?" he mumbles, looking at Tucker. "Was anybody else there?"

I never really thought about who else was inside the house that day. But now with my brain half awake and half asleep, I do remember someone being there.

"Sister Grimes," I say, surprising myself with the memory. "Sister Grimes was in the kitchen." Holy crap. I have to be sure to tell Frank this the next time I see him.

Mordecai cocks his head at me. "Sister Grimes?"

"She's a gossip who goes to North Creek Church of God," I say, looking him square in the eyes. They seem different now. They're not cold and scary-looking anymore.

"Becky Grimes?"

I nod. "She threatened Mama at the church potluck a few months before that," I say.

"Threatened?" Mordecai glances away from me real fast and looks at Tucker, scratching him on the head again. It makes him look shifty. "What did she say exactly?"

I should probably tell him that I don't remember because of self-incrimination.

Self-incrimination is when you say something real dumb by accident that links you to a crime and then you're screwed.

But I do remember now. Like it was yesterday. I can hear her saying it in my head just like she said it while I was playing hide-and-seek with the preacher's daughter, Lily. Sister Grimes didn't know I was hiding under the dessert table while she stood there gossiping with the preacher's wife.

It'll kill Carolyn if she finds out that boy is funny.

I knew she was talking about me. She always looked at me with raised eyebrows when I played with Lily and her American Girl dolls at church potlucks instead of playing softball with the other boys. And I'm sure Gene told her all about the Coat Cubby Serial Kisser of Buckingham Elementary.

"I don't know," I lie, handing him the empty water bottle. "I don't remember. Shouldn't we keep going? It's getting late, right?"

Mordecai does that hairy eye squint-stare thing at me again, like he knows I'm lying. But he doesn't ask anything more about Sister Grimes. He stands, glances up at the sky, and then points forward. "This way. Not too much farther."

He leads Tucker and me for a while longer, humming Billy Joel the whole time. I kind of recognize the melody. Mama knew all the Billy Joel songs and sang them a lot. I bet I would know it if he sang the words, but I'm not about to ask him to sing. We just walk and walk and walk. Could be fifteen minutes, could be fifty. Heck if I know. But we need to hurry. This might be my last chance to find the Whispers and save Mama. And it looks like the sun will be setting soon.

We walk some more. And then some more. My legs ache and my stomach growls. Tucker slugs along getting slower and slower. Finally Mordecai has mercy on us and stops.

"This is as far as I can take you." He reaches into his canvas satchel, pulls out another bottle of water, and hands it to me.

I look up at him. "Why? Are you scared of the Whispers?"

He kind of chuckle-grunts. "It's not your Whispers I'm worried about. The north tree line ain't far past the beaver dam. I like to keep my distance from the world beyond it. They don't like me out there, and to be honest, I don't care much for how they treat each other." He points with his whole arm. "Just keep walking thataway. The beaver dam's not far. You can't miss it. Keep walking in the same direction past that and you'll find your way home." He lowers his head and stares at the ground or at Tucker. I can't tell which. "I'll hang back, but I'll keep an eye on you until you're out of the woods. Make sure you get there okay."

I stare at Mordecai and search for words. I think about the sad run-down shack he lives in all alone. About the way people have talked about him all these years and the horrible stuff they say he did. How he looked me in the eye and told me he never hurt anyone and I believe him. And how he knew my mama and that she was one of the only people who was kind to him. But I don't think Mordecai cares about any of that anymore. Right now he only cares about helping me find Mama. That he's helping a little boy lost in the woods—doing the opposite of what the outside world thinks he would do. Doing the opposite of what a hobgoblin would do.

"If you see Dylan again, will you tell him I'm okay?" I ask, not knowing what else to say.

He glances down at me, his whole beard curling up into a smile. "And that I didn't eat you?"

I smile at him. "Yeah. Thanks for that."

I think that's all that needs to be said, so I nod at him, smile, and nudge Tucker in the direction of the beaver dam. I don't look back at Mordecai until he calls out my name. I stop and turn to face him.

He stands there a ways behind me with his arms crossed over his chest. "I'm sure your mama misses you just as much as you miss her. Go find her."

For some reason a huge lump clogs my throat, my eyes start itching, and I can't say anything. Wouldn't know what to say if I could. Not only that, but I'm really hungry, and I'm so tired I could sit down right here on the ground and cry. Mama says sometimes you just get so tired and plumb wore out with everything that you need a good cry to wash all the bad stuff out of your insides. But I don't have time for that right now, so instead I wave goodbye to Mordecai and march off with Tucker to find the Whispers. And Mama.

23

THE BEAVER DAM

Mordecai was right. It didn't take me long to find the beaver dam. The sound of rushing water led me right to the creek where a huge wall of sticks and branches blocks the flow of water. I can't imagine how long it took the beavers to build this thing, but now I understand what Grandma means when she says she's *busy as a beaver*. She ain't lying.

Tucker laps up water from the creek, then goes over to a nearby tree and vomits it right back up. I kneel next to him and rub his head—my stomach twisting in knots. He's panting really heavy through a toothy smile. I know he doesn't want me to worry about him.

"It's okay, Tuck. You'll be all right."

He looks up at me with those huge, dark eyes of his and whimpers, like he's embarrassed. Tucker's never been one to make a fuss about anything, even when he's sick. And he hates leaving a mess anywhere, but sometimes he can't help it. I scratch behind his ear and search the bank of the creek. A tree stump sits near the dam, almost as if it was put there so you could sit and study the handiwork of the beavers. I drag myself over to it, Tucker lumbering and panting beside me. My legs are numb and my eyes are heavy with needed sleep. If I can just sit for a few minutes and rest, I'll be in better shape to help Mama when I find her.

My butt hits the ground with a plop and I lean against the stump. Tucker lies down right beside me and rests his big Rottie head on my leg, looking thankful for the break. He closes his eyes and less than a minute later he's snoring like Grandma does on the sofa after a pill-box dessert. Tucker doesn't need pills, though. He can fall asleep on a dime whenever he wants to. He's like a robot shutting down for temporary maintenance or something. That would be pretty cool if Tucker was really a cyborg dog, and actually it would explain a lot. Like how smart and huge and perfect-looking he is. Then he could live forever.

Resting my head against the stump, listening to the water trickle through holes in the dam, I drink the last of the water Mordecai gave me. My eyelids feel like they're made of concrete. If I could just close them for five minutes . . .

Mama sits on the swing on the back porch, watching me direct the Pentecostal corn choir. She just got home from her shift at the hospital and says she's too tired to join me, but she'll watch, so we give her a private concert. We open with "Amazing Grace," followed by "Blessed Assurance," and then close with her favorite hymn, "It Is Well with My Soul."

Mama lies on her and Daddy's bed, taking a nap. Thankfully she finally quit the temp job at the hospital, but she's still tired a lot because she has a real bad flu or something. I guess I accidentally wake her, because she sits up.

"What time is it, Button?" she says, looking at me.

Her hair is weird and her face is pale. This flu has really done a number on her.

"It's six thirty," I say.

"Did Grandma bring you boys some supper?" she asks. "Is your daddy home yet?"

She stands up and walks toward me. That's when I see it. The Windy City Slasher's butcher knife lying on the bed. I panic. I'm having the dream again and I'm stuck in it. I can't wake myself up this time, hard as I try. I feel like I'm drowning in an ocean of sleep.

"Hurry, Mama."

It's all I can get out, but she doesn't walk any faster. She's tired. The knife floats up off the bed and hangs in midair, pointing right at her back.

"Mama, please hurry!" I yell, but it's like she's walking in slow motion now. Wake up. Wake up. Wake up.

"Mama!" I try to run to her, but my feet are glued to the floor and I can't move them. My breath catches in my throat. I reach out to

Mama with both hands just as the Windy City Slasher's knife sails through the air at her.

I wake up screaming.

Tucker lifts his head with a start, ears pointing straight up to Jesus. He stares at me with that *was it the nightmare again, dude?* look on his face.

A soft buzz in my ear startles me. I scramble to my feet and spin around hoping it's not a moth. But then it's gone. The light in the woods has dimmed quite a bit. How long was I asleep? Five minutes? Five days? Heck if I know.

I scan the treetops but can't really tell where the sun is. It might've set already. What if I missed them? I walk over to the edge of the creek, kneel down, and splash water on my face. It's cold and stings my skin in a good way. I have to stay awake.

I look up. A lone beaver with a stick in his mouth trots along the top of the dam, not even giving me a second look. He goes back and forth over one area until he finds the spot he wants and places the stick carefully. Beavers have a lot of perseverance.

Perseverance is when you're able to wait for something without getting your panties all in a wad.

Like, *You need some real perseverance to build a dam one stick at a time.*

Riley.

I spin around in the direction of the tiny voice, but I

can't tell which direction it came from. Something grazes my arm and I scramble back over to the stump. Tucker sits up on his haunches and sniffs the air like he smells them. I take a deep breath and wait. Watch. Listen.

Riley.

I look all around for them, but the voices are everywhere. The evening concert by nature's symphony begins, making it even harder to pinpoint where they are. I close my eyes and imagine the Whispers dancing to the music as if part of the performance. Another slight brush on the rim of my ear makes me open my eyes again.

One by one, they slip through the back door of my imagination and out into the real world. I see them—the floating blue lights, fading in and out, and suddenly they're everywhere. One right next to me, only a few inches away. One drifting through the air on the other side of the creek. Two to my right, another on my left, weaving in and out of the treetops and then appearing out of nowhere right in front of my face. Once I set my eyes on one Whisper, it disappears. It's like they're playing hide-and-seek with me or want me to chase them. I stay perfectly still and in no time flat they multiply five times over. I can't believe how many there are now—maybe hundreds, maybe thousands. They leave trails of shimmering blue light. Little blue fairies, just like Mordecai said—it's beautiful and magical.

Tucker suddenly comes alive, jumping around trying to catch them in his mouth. I don't think he's trying to eat them, but without hands it's his only way to grab at them.

"Tucker, no!"

He doesn't listen to me. He follows them down the bank of the creek, stomping at the ones flying close to the ground with his giant paws. I'm actually more worried about Tucker than the Whispers. They could have magical zapping powers or something that could reduce Tucker to ashes or fry his cyborg dog motherboard and paralyze him forever if he makes them angry.

"Tucker!"

He looks back at me and freezes for a second, his panting on overdrive.

I point my finger at him and give him a stern look. "No!"

He whines and eyes the Whispers zooming around his head, but he stops snapping at them with his huge cyborg dog jaws of death. I put a finger to my lips, motioning for him to be quiet. Nature's symphony gets louder, drawing even more Whispers out into the open to join in the production. Now is my chance. But with Grandpa's Swiss Army knife and Mama's wedding ring gone, I don't have a tribute left to give them. Maybe they'll understand.

I go over to the stump and stand behind it like it's the preacher's podium at North Creek Church of God. Clearing my throat, I give Tucker one more silent warning, pointing my finger at him. He sits there a few feet way, panting hard with his whole body and looking anxious, but obeying. I watch the swarm of Whispers in front of me. I'm not afraid to look directly at them now because I have nothing else to lose. Not even hope.

"I gave you everything I have," I say in a surprisingly loud and clear voice. "My grandpa's antique Swiss Army knife and my mama's wedding ring. You told me she was here. So, where is she?"

A honeysuckle-scented breeze rolls over the creek like a fragrant ocean wave. I listen carefully, trying to weed out any sound other than the voices of the Whispers. A soft, wispy word buzzes in my ear.

Tribute.

"I don't have any more tributes!" I kind of shout it. I'm tired and angry. And I want this to be over.

Soul.

The word rings in my ears. Tucker becomes agitated and growls at them. He doesn't move or pounce, but I guess he can understand them because he doesn't like what they just said.

I sigh, all patience gone. "My soul? How the heck do I even do that? What about my family? I couldn't do that to them."

I hope the Whispers don't call my bluff. Honestly my family would be just fine without me. They'd probably be better off not having to see the face of the person responsible for Mama's disappearance staring back at them every day.

I look around, wondering if Mordecai really is out there somewhere keeping an eye on me like he said he would. If he is, I could really use his help right now.

"This isn't a game," I say, louder and with an edge to my voice. It's not what I'd planned to say, but I feel like I'm channeling Detective Chase Cooper, bargaining with the perp. "A woman could be in danger. She needs help. Take me to her now and I'll never bother you ever again."

The Whispers fill the air, their soft blue glow fading in and out like the heartbeat of the entire woods. Tucker is surrounded and edges back nervously.

A single tiny voice tickles my ear. *Soul.*

"I can't!" My voice echoes through the trees, releasing Mama's forbidden word from my lips. Its sting lingers on my tongue. "I can't give you my soul. I don't know how."

You're close.

She's close.

My heart nearly pounds its way right through my shirt. "Mama?" I whisper back.

Carolyn.

Mama.

I don't understand how to give the Whispers my soul as a tribute, or what would happen to me if I did. Would I really become like them and have to stay with them here in the woods forever like the story says? But . . . I don't care anymore. If that's what it takes to find Mama, it's worth it. She can come visit me in the woods and I can whisper to her through the wind every evening during magic time. It won't be exactly the same as having a real mama, but it'll be better than having no mama at all.

"Okay," I say in a loud and steady voice. "I'll give you my soul. Show me how. Please. Show me."

Tears stream cold down my cheeks and sobs of

exhaustion and desperation force me to my knees. I shake all over. I'm cold and I feel like I'm crumbling into a million pieces. I don't know what's happening to me. The sobbing takes over my whole body in heaving waves of sorrow. I can't control it or hold it in. I've never cried like this before, but now I can't stop. Maybe this is how the Whispers take your soul. Maybe your soul pours out of you in an ocean of tears. Maybe that's where your soul lives—in your tears.

But it doesn't bring Mama back. I cry out every tear of my soul for the Whispers, but she doesn't come. They lied to me. *The Whispers lied.*

I scramble to my feet and scream, swatting at them with both hands, but I can barely see through all the soul pouring out of my eyes. This gets Tucker going again and he joins me in my war on the Whispers as best he can.

"You said she was here! You lied to me! I hate you!"

I reach into my pockets and pull out the only thing in there. The note and the ten-dollar bill Daddy left me. I rip them both to shreds and throw the pieces in the air. The breeze scoops them up and scatters them everywhere.

"Here," I scream. "Now you have it all. You've taken everything from me."

Pieces of the note and money land on the bank and some in the creek, floating away downstream like regular old trash. My final tribute means nothing to the Whispers.

There are less of them by the second now. Fading away into the shadows. They're leaving. One of them flutters by my ear. I slap at it, grabbing the creature and holding it tight in my fist. I can feel its tiny wings struggle against my skin, but not for long. I crush it with all the pain bottled inside me. I crush it for lying to me. I crush it because Daddy doesn't love me anymore. I crush it because God ignored everyone's prayers. I crush it because I'll never find Mama. I crush it because there's something wrong with me. I crush it dead.

I scream one more time at my balled-up fist. Tucker whimpers behind me, but I don't look at him. I just stare at my fist like a crazy person. My knuckles are white and I feel dizzy. I ease my grip and slow my breathing before I pass out. Peeling back my fingers one by one, I gaze down into my palm at the tiny crushed corpse.

The creature's blue glow fades one last time, like a final breath before it dies, and now I see the Whisper for what it really is. It's not a fairy. It's not made of skin and bones like me, or of tree bark, or leaves, or dirt. It's not beautiful and it's not magical. It's a bug. It's just a bug.

A loud crack of thunder sounds in the distance, stopping the sobs cold in my throat. Tucker barks like he's answering the call. But it wasn't thunder exactly. It was something else that sounded familiar. The blast of a shotgun. My mind races.

Dylan.

Oh, no. What if Dylan shot Mordecai, thinking he did something to hurt me? Or what if Danny shot Dylan, or Gary, or Carl, thinking they were squirrels?

Another shot cracks the sky and the echo gets carried off by the breeze.

Tucker answers the blast with an urgent bark. He trots off through the woods in the direction of the gunfire.

"Tucker! No!"

But he's gone. I run after him, still clutching the dead bug in my right hand. Tucker's not running full blast, but I'm so tired, I still can't keep up with him. I just follow the sound of his barking.

"Tucker!"

Tripping over a branch, I hit the ground face first—*hard*. My knee stings and the side of my face burns. I struggle to get back up to my feet, but I'm so tired it takes me a minute to get my bearings again. Tucker's bark is even farther away now. A cold Mountain Dew and some Funyuns would really give me the strength I need right now. But thinking about food or sleep isn't going to help.

After a few more minutes of getting whacked in the face by tree limbs and tripping over branches, I finally break through the tree line and stumble out into a wide-open area. My eyes are blurry with sweat, tears, and the dusky twilight, but what I see doesn't make any sense.

How did I get here?

Maybe I'm dreaming. That's got to be it. This was all a dream. I'll wake up any second in my own pee-soaked bed. That actually sounds nice right about now. I know there's a six-pack of Mountain Dew in the fridge and Danny probably has a bag of Funyuns hidden somewhere in his room.

But that would also mean that the Whispers were just a dream. Mordecai being a nice human person and not a scary hobgoblin was just a dream. And the most perfect moment in the history of moments last night with Dylan was a dream too. Maybe everything was a dream.

My eyes refuse to stay open a second longer. My spaghetti legs give out from under me and one question rattles around in my foggy brain as I hit the ground.

Was Mama just a dream?

24

CAROLYN RILEY JAMES

My face is warm. The rest of me feels pretty warm too, and I smell *real* bad. A pinch of pain from the crick in my neck sparks my eyes open. The world is sunlit, sideways, and strange. Not too far away, a large pointy structure rests on its side, the sun peeking out from behind it. There're no more trees. There's grass. And flowers. And dewy morning air.

Something is draped over me like a blanket. It's warm, but it smells like man sweat and armpits. I touch the faded blue denim fabric. *Mordecai's shirt.* He must have carried me here all the way from the tree line. I guess he was looking out for me after all.

A heavy weight presses against my back. I turn over and see that it's Tucker. His furry back is nestled up against me just like he used to do when he slept in the bed with me before *my condition* started.

My condition.

I sit up in a start and check my pants, but to my surprise, they're bone-dry. Not even a drop of stray pee anywhere.

I slept here all the way through the night and didn't wet myself. But where the heck is here?

A few feet away, a large stone with a curved top sticks out of the ground. There's another one sort of like it to the right and more of them to the left, all different shapes and sizes. Some have crosses on them and some have fake or dying flowers planted in front of them. I look over at the pointy structure, which has now righted itself since I'm sitting up, and it finally clicks in my sleep-drunk brain. I'm in the cemetery behind North Creek Church of God.

I nudge Tucker with my elbow. "Tuck. Wake up." He doesn't move. Doesn't stir. And he's not snoring.

"Tucker?"

His rib cage isn't moving up and down like it usually does when he sleeps either. Panic rises up from the pit of my stomach as I scramble around to face him. My heart drops. His eyes are open but they're cold and lifeless.

"Tucker! Tucker, wake up, boy," I say, shaking him, my throat closing up on me. "It's okay, boy. It's okay. Everything's okay now." My eyes instantly fill with tears, though I didn't think I had any left inside me. "Please, Tucker. Please don't leave me. Please don't leave me. Please don't leave me."

I repeat it like a prayer, but Tucker doesn't move. Just stares straight past me. His eyes don't see me anymore. He's not in there. God's still not hearing my prayers or He still doesn't care. Wrapping my arms around Tucker's big furry body, I pull him into my lap. Bury my face in the soft fur of his neck and sob.

"Why here, Tuck? I don't want to be here. Not here. Anywhere but here."

I sit like that for a while, sobbing into his fur and rocking the lifeless body of the greatest dog in the history of dogs. My protector. My friend.

Through eyes blurred by tears, I finally look up and stare at the headstone right in front of me, the one I'd slept under all night and the one Tucker had died under. I read the name engraved in the stone in fancy, pointy letters.

Carolyn Riley James

Mama's name. My name. A name we share. Like Danny shares Daddy's name. Engraved under her name are the day and month of the birthday we share, the year Mama was born, and another date about four months ago. It was the last time I was here. Her funeral. Near the bottom of the headstone are four words that kick-start my spotty memory into high gear.

Good Night, My Love

I hold Tucker tight, my soul pouring out of my eyes again as I gently stroke his fur. I hum the song to him, the one Mama wrote for me. I remember it now. All of it. Mama getting weak and sicker by the day, the chemo treatments at Upton Hospital—not a temp job; her beautiful wavy hair getting thin and falling out; the night she died—Danny and I were staying over at Grandma and Grandpa's when Daddy called; Grandma's terrifying screams and wailing—

she sounded like a wild animal dying; Grandpa sobbing in his recliner—I'd never seen him cry in my entire life; the wake at our house, Mama laid out in the casket in the living room—not napping on the sofa; Sister Grimes and the preacher's wife in Mama's kitchen arranging all the food everyone brought; the funeral at North Creek Church of God packed with people. I remember everything, even though I don't want to. All the memories are released into my brain from the dark corner where I'd kept them locked up all these months. I don't look away, though; I keep stroking Tucker's fur, humming Mama's lullaby to him, and set the real memories free.

"Riley!"

Hearing my name being called out from the tree line confuses me. It doesn't sound like the Whispers, and now I know they aren't real anyway. But I recognize the voice the second time it calls out to me.

I look back to the tree line. Dylan runs toward me, two backpacks over his shoulder and his shotgun hanging at his side. I rest my chin on Tucker's head and stare at Mama's name carved in the headstone. She's never coming back. Because of me.

"Riley?" The drum of Dylan's footsteps stops a few feet away from me. "Are you okay? I've been looking for you since yesterday. Your daddy too. I went and told him that I couldn't find you. He's worried sick. I was hoping you'd hear the shots I fired."

I look back at him. I see now that he's carrying my Black

Panther backpack as well as his own. He's staring at Tucker with widened eyes.

"He's dead," I say, through a sob that catches in my throat. I swallow it back. "She's dead too." I nod to Mama's headstone. "I killed her."

Dylan drops the backpacks, lays the shotgun on the ground, and runs over to me. He squats down in front of me like an adult would.

"I'm so sorry, Riley." He pets Tucker's head and his eyes mist over instantly. Soon tears flow out of his eyes as easily as they do mine. Suddenly Dylan seems more a boy like me than an adult or a superhero. He glances up at Mama's headstone and wipes his nose with the back of his hand. "But you didn't kill her. Why would you say something like that?" His voice fades away and cracks at the end.

There was a time when I would have been too embarrassed or ashamed to tell Dylan about *my other condition*. But I don't care anymore. I don't care about anything anymore.

"Sister Grimes said so," I say, steadying my voice.

"What the heck are you talking about?" His superhero voice is back but the tears still slip out.

I wipe my eyes with the smelly sleeve of Mordecai's shirt. "Sister Grimes said it would kill Mama if she found out I was funny. And then Mama caught me kissing Kenny from Kentucky in Daddy's work shed. She got sick soon after that, and then she did die, just like Sister Grimes said she would."

Dylan has a soft look in his wet eyes. He doesn't respond to my confession the way I thought he would. He doesn't seem shocked or grossed out by it. He doesn't call me a pervert or run away from me or punch me in the face. He actually does something so unexpected that it makes me start crying all over again. He sits beside me, leaning his back on Mama's headstone. Gently pressing my head to his chest, he pulls me close to him, wrapping his superhero arms tight around me, and we just sit there while I cry out what's left of my soul. Dylan holding me. Me holding Tucker. And Mama holding us all.

A long time passes before Dylan says anything, which is fine with me, because sitting there with my head resting on his chest and his arms wrapped around me is hands-down the most loved I've felt since Mama disappeared. Since Mama died. Finally my sobs ease up and the only sounds I hear now are the beat of Dylan's heart in one ear and the birds waking up in the other.

"She just died, Riley," Dylan says in a breathy whisper on my ear.

Normally my internal Charlie Brown teacher translator would kick in whenever someone said something like that, but it isn't working anymore. I hear the words loud and clear. *She just died.*

"And it wasn't because she saw you kissing a boy. She was real sick. She had cancer. She went for chemo at the Upton Hospital for months, but it just didn't work. And that's not your fault. It's not anyone's fault. It just is. And it's okay to cry because it sucks. My mama died the same way when I was real little."

And then the King of the Redneck Superheroes does something that warms me from head to toe. He kisses me right on the top of my head. Just like Daddy did when he used to love me.

"Come on, I'll take you home, and you can come back with your daddy to get Tucker." Dylan moves his hand from my chest, and when he does, something makes a crinkling sound in Mordecai's shirt. I look down and slip my hand into the chest pocket.

"Where'd that shirt come from?" Dylan asks. "It reeks."

"Mordecai Mathews," I say as I pull out the Ziploc bag that I'd dropped in the clearing.

"Mordie?" Dylan says, surprised and then alarmed. "Did he hurt you?"

I want to say, *No. The hobgoblin is actually a nice human person and I think he was falsely accused because Mama believed him and I do too and it's terrible the way everyone treats him.*

But I don't. I can't stop staring at the contents of the Ziploc bag, the Magic Markered word PRIVATE only slightly blocking my view of Grandpa's Swiss Army knife and Mama's wedding ring.

25

THE WORST BROTHER IN THE HISTORY OF BROTHERS?

Later that day, we all stand quietly under the shade of the old oak tree in the backyard—me, Daddy, Grandpa, Grandma, and Danny. I was so tired when I got home this morning that after I took a shower, I collapsed on my bed and was out for most of the day. I didn't pee on the bed, though. I think I've been cured of *my condition.* Daddy finally came in and woke me up because it was time. I called Gary's mom and invited him and Carl, but they didn't show. I think I totally ruined my friendship with Gary.

I guess most dog person funerals aren't normally well attended, because this is nothing like Mama's at the North Creek Church of God. That day the church was packed to the gills with people and flowers. Every seat was taken and people stood in the back and all along the side aisles. I think all of Buckingham *and* Upton came out to pay their respects. Gary and Carl were there with their mama and daddy, Mr. and Mrs. Killen, too. Everybody from church came, just like it was Easter Sunday morning and not just a regular Sunday. Some of my teachers from school and Miss

Betty came, Mama's beauty pageant friends, Miss Sandy, and some of the nurses from the Upton Hospital Cancer Treatment Center. Poor families Mama had helped along the way showed up too, and families of prisoners she visited and became friends with. Even Dylan Mathews and his father came and stood in the very back of the church like a couple of statues.

I'd never seen so many flowers in one place at one time either. You couldn't even see the altars for all of the colorful arrangements. A lot of red roses. Everyone knew Mama loved red roses. The church choir sang Mama's favorite hymn, "It Is Well with My Soul," and then the preacher talked about all of Mama's *Christian virtues*, her charity work with the *indigent and the incarcerated*, her *uncommon beauty both inside and out*, and how only Jesus knew why he needed to *take her home to glory at such a young age*, with so much life in front of her and leaving two young boys without a mama and a young man without the love of his life. *Ours was not to ask why*, he'd said, *but to trust in the Lord*. But I've always had a problem not asking why. It's like my favorite question ever. Maybe that's why God doesn't like to listen to my prayers. Because I ask Him why—like *a lot*.

I remember sitting on the very front pew just a few feet from the casket, between Daddy and Grandma, being suffocated by their grief. Grandma sobbing loudly while squeezing my right hand so tight I thought she might break it off, and Daddy's whole body drawn in on itself, weeping silently into his hands and shaking all over. It was awful.

Especially when Grandma started wailing like a dying animal when they lowered Mama's casket into the ground in the graveyard behind the church. I didn't cry that day because there wasn't any room left for my tears. I just kept looking back and forth from Grandma to Daddy and holding Mama's ring tight in my left hand, tucked deep inside my suit coat pocket. I knew it was too late to put it back in the casket with her and I knew I could never tell anyone I took it the day before, during the wake at our house. That's what really happened. And I guess that's when my head and my heart got together and decided I couldn't take any more of all the crying, screaming, and wailing. So they told me a different story. A story that wouldn't be so terrible as all that. A story with hope. But I don't think my head and my heart meant any harm. They were just looking out for me, so I forgive them.

Daddy slings the last of the loose dirt on Tucker's grave and pats it down gently with the back of the shovel. We're all silent, and I wonder if somebody should say something. Or sing. If Mama were here, she'd sing a hymn, but none of us can sing as good as her. Besides, I don't know any dog person hymns. I'm sure they have them because people say all dogs go to heaven. I think dogs are automatic Christians from the day they're born until the day they die, with a one-way ticket straight to heaven. No dumb rules like the ones they teach at the North Creek Church of God, because dogs don't know how to sin. All they know how to do is love. They forgive and forget easily, they don't hold grudges, and they lie down and take a nap whenever they're tired. We should all be more like dogs. I know I'll never be as great as Tucker, but I'm gonna try to live by his example. I might even just lie right down on the floor in Mrs. Turner's class and take a nap if I get tired. Then again, I'm afraid she might go all *DC Fixer* Cassandra Bailey on my butt.

Grandpa has his arm around Grandma and they're both smiling through tears. Danny hangs his head, so I can't tell if he's crying or not. Me, I don't have any tears left in me. I'm all cried out. I feel kind of numb all over, the way I did at Mama's funeral four months ago.

Daddy has a sad look on his face, but when he's done shoveling, he comes over, stands by me, and puts his arm around my shoulders. He was so glad to see me when Dylan brought me home this morning that I thought he was going to cry. He didn't even yell at me for lying to him about staying over at Gary's house. Just grabbed me and hugged me the way he used to before Mama died. It was weird, and nice, and familiar all at the same time.

He looks down at me, his eyes softer than I've seen them in a long, long time. "You want to say anything, son?"

Son. He hasn't called me that in like forever.

I take a step forward and stand at the foot of Tucker's grave. Daddy made him a wooden cross and carved his name on it. We buried him beside *Can't* and *If,* which makes sense because I don't think Tucker would have even known those two words if he spoke human. He could do anything and never made excuses.

I open my mouth to speak, but stop when I spot two familiar figures coming around the side of the house. They walk over to us slowly, real respectful-like, and stand beside Danny. Gary nods at me and Carl hangs his head like he's praying. I give Gary a little smile, but not too much because I don't want to scare him off before I have a chance to apologize to him. I nod back, silently thanking him for coming.

Clearing my throat, I start again. "Just like Mama, Tucker taught me a lot of stuff. He didn't worry about what happened yesterday or what might happen tomorrow; he just made the best of right now and he wasn't afraid to face it head-on. And he always saw the good in people, no matter what other people said about them." I look over at Gary. "He never let his friends down either and he was never mean to them. He loved everyone unconditionally. Like Mama did. I need to be more like Tucker. And Mama."

I step back. I know it was short and Tucker deserves better, but I did the best I could. I think he knows that.

Gary sort of smiles at me. Danny picks up a handful of dirt and tosses it on top of the grave. I finally see his eyes. They're wet and he sniffles a little. Gary and Carl do the same thing Danny did, picking up some loose dirt and throwing it on the grave. I do too.

Grandpa says a closing prayer but cuts it short when he starts getting choked up. I'm still not sure God is listening, though. I want to believe He is. I'd like to think He's taking care of Mama and Tucker up in heaven. Giving them the tour, showing them the ropes, and not getting too mad at

Tucker when he poops on the streets of gold. Tucker hates leaving a mess.

After the *Amens*, Daddy squeezes my shoulder and goes to put the shovel back in the shed. I walk over to Gary.

"Hey," I say. *Lame.*

"'Sup," Gary says back.

"Thanks for coming," I say. *Lame times two.*

He just nods and looks down. Carl stares up at me with a hard look on his face. I guess he didn't like how I treated his big brother any more than I did.

"Look, dude," I say. "I'm really, really, *really* sorry for those things I said in the woods."

Gary looks up. "Me too."

I smile at him. "And thanks."

"For what?" he says, scrunching up his face at me.

"For helping me find her," I say.

Gary shrugs. "I didn't do anything."

"I know you didn't believe in the Whispers or that we could find Mama," I say. "But you went along with it anyway. For me. So thanks."

Gary stares at me for a long moment and then does something I'm not expecting. He grabs me and hugs me. A big, hard hug. It's awkward and nice all at the same time.

"It's all good, dawg," he says with that huge smile of his. "See you on the bus."

I walk Gary and Carl to the dirt road that runs in front of our house and they head back home. An old pickup truck stirs up dust and dirt as it rambles in my direction. A hand sticks out of the window and waves at Gary and Carl as it passes them. They wave back. When the truck reaches me, it stops. It's one of those old-timey blue Fords with lots of curves and dents and places to stand on the side. Dylan is behind the steering wheel in a plain white T-shirt and his Peterbilt ball cap, looking like an adult again. I know he's about a year shy of being legally old enough to drive with a learner's permit because he's the same age as Danny. But as long as he sticks to the back roads of Buckingham County, nobody around here cares about all them city rules.

I walk over to the truck and he smiles at me through the rolled-downed window as he kills the rumbling engine. It coughs and hacks and finally sputters off.

"Hey," I say. *Lame the sequel.*

"Hey, Riley," he says.

His face is looking a little better, but the damage is still visible. I wonder if the bruises his daddy gave him will ever go away or if they'll be a part of Dylan forever.

"You all right?"

I nod real fast. I don't know why.

"That's cool," he says.

Dylan Mathews said I was cool. Sort of.

"We just buried Tucker," I say, like we're talking about the weather or something. "Grandma made his favorite. Angel food cake. Want some?"

I hold my breath. I hope he doesn't think I meant *like a date* or anything. I know Dylan's too old for me. And he probably wants to kiss girls instead of boys. I can't understand why, but I've never kissed a girl, so who am I to judge?

Dylan rests his wrist on top of the steering wheel, peers straight ahead, and then checks his rearview mirror before turning his gaze back on me.

"Nah," he says. "I gotta get going."

He must see the disappointment on my face.

"Thanks, though," he says with a smile. "Angel food cake is my favorite, too."

I stand on my tiptoes and peek inside the cab of the truck like a nosy gossip would do. Dylan's backpack is in there on the seat. So is a large duffel bag.

"Where you going?"

Eyes back to the front windshield. "Up the road a bit to stay with my aunt for a while."

Eyes back to me. It's like he knew that news would disappoint me, so he didn't want to look at me when he said it.

"I won't be on the bus," he says. "But I'll still see you at school."

A flood of relief relaxes me again. I hear my name being yelled a ways behind me. I turn and see that it's my brother standing by the side of the house.

"Grandma said come on, the cake's ready," Danny hollers. He doesn't have any manners.

Dylan waves at Danny and Danny waves back. I guess they knew each other in another life—before Dylan was held back a grade and before Danny became a horrible high school person.

"Go eat your cake and have some for me," Dylan says like an adult as he starts up the engine again. "And say goodbye to Tucker for me."

Before he leaves, he reaches out the window and hands me a small slip of paper. I take it, confused. I'm sure it's not a love note or anything, though.

I unfold it real quick and read the three words Dylan wrote.

"Look it up," he says, smiling and with a little wave as he slowly pulls away.

I wave back, watching his truck until it gets all the way to the end of the dirt road, turning right and disappearing out of sight. I feel a little embarrassed for staring at Dylan's truck so long when I turn around and find Danny walking up to me. I stuff the slip of paper down into my pocket.

"Come on," he says with that usual Danny edge to his voice. "Everybody's waitin' for you and I want some cake."

I huff as I pass him, a little ticked that he cut short my visit with Dylan.

"Hey, wait," he says, touching my shoulder.

I stop and turn to face him. "What?" It comes out sounding just like a regular question. I don't do rude voice as well as Danny does. It must just come naturally to him.

He pulls something out of the back pocket of his jeans. "I wanted to give this to you."

"Huh?" Also lame, but I'm hearing words that don't make any sense together coming out of Danny's mouth.

He holds something out to me and I take it. When I look

down at it, my eyes start itching again. Maybe there're some tears and some soul left in me after all. It's the picture of Mama riding on the back of the open Mustang convertible in the Christmas parade when she was a contestant in the Mrs. Upton pageant. I stare at it, at her, waving to me on the sidewalk with her big smile and queenly wave.

"I know you always liked that one," Danny says, peering over my shoulder.

I turn and give him a look of shock, disbelief, and gratitude all at once.

Gratitude is just like when you're really, really super thankful for something.

Like, *I have a feeling Danny is going to hold this gratitude I'm feeling over my head for the rest of my life.*

"I know you found them," he says. "The photo albums. I wasn't trying to keep them from you. I just . . . I don't know. You had her all the time. I just wanted her to myself for a little while."

I stare at his face like I don't recognize it anymore. I know my gratitude is supposed to make me say something like, *Wow, Danny. Thank you SO much. You're like the best big brother in the whole world.*

But the thought of saying that makes me want to throw up in my mouth a little. So instead I say, "How did you know I found them?"

He rolls his eyes at me. "You didn't put them back the way I had them. And I know you have her ring. I found it in your drawer the other day. I knew you were hiding something in there and I was mad that you went snooping around in my room."

It takes me a couple of seconds to understand what he's saying, but it finally settles down in my brain. "It was you," I say. *And not the Whispers,* I don't say.

He nods toward the house like I should follow him. "Don't worry, I didn't tell Daddy about the ring."

I follow him, staring at the picture of Mama and not my feet, so I stumble a couple of times. Danny walks a couple steps in front of me like he has our whole lives.

"You can look at them anytime you want, you know," he says. "Just knock first and no more snooping when I'm not home."

I stare up at the back of his head and for once in my life I don't know what to say to him. Gratitude is a powerful drug. I feel like I'm high on the devil's weed, whatever that feels like.

Maybe Danny's not the worst brother in the history of brothers after all.

26

PUTTIN' ON AIRS

A few days later I sit on Frank's Fritos-smelling couch for what I hope will be the last time ever. Frank sits across from me, tapping away on his iPad. I look over at the triangle-shaped nameplate on his still messy and still unprofessional-looking desk.

Frank Harvey, PhD

Turns out Frank wasn't puttin' on airs by using three names. The third name wasn't even a name, although Grandma might say that letting everyone know you're a doctor with a sign on your door *and* on your desk is kind of puttin' on airs.

I glance above Frank's head at the large framed certificates hanging on the wall behind him. They're from the University of South Carolina and have CHILD PSYCHOLOGY written on them in big, swirly letters. One is proof that Frank is an actual real doctor. The other is proof that Frank has another degree in being a bachelor. No surprise there.

"Very interesting," Frank finally says, holding up the slip of paper Dylan gave me before he left.

The note has the words *Blue Ghost Fireflies* written on it in redneck superhero handwriting.

"Seems your friend Dylan was correct."

My friend Dylan. I really like the sound of that.

Frank turns the iPad around so I can see what he found. An article on blue ghost fireflies fills the screen. There's a picture with the article that shows several of the creatures up close, glowing with their beautiful fairy-blue light.

"I didn't know there were different kinds of fireflies." Frank turns the iPad back to face him. "They glow a soft blue light instead of flashing a yellow-green one like normal lightning bugs. Fascinating."

I look at him and cock my head. "They're not *not* normal. They're just different."

"Of course." Frank puts down the iPad and rests his hands in a ball on top of his big belly. "So let's go through it one last time, Riley."

I manage to stop myself from rolling my eyes at him, but I imagine doing it, which is almost as good.

"Mama was sick," I say. "She died of cancer, just like Tucker did."

Frank nods, encouraging me to continue.

I sigh a little, but not overly disrespectful-like. "We had her wake at our house. They laid her out in the living room. Moved the nice sofa out and put the casket where it usually goes. The two men waiting outside by the big white car were from Graham Funeral Home."

"And where were you during the visitation, Riley?"

I fidget with my shoelaces and shift in my seat. My voice comes out shaky. "Outside playing with Gary and Carl."

Frank cocks his head at me. "Something about that makes you uncomfortable, Riley. What is it?"

I don't like Frank right now. But the sooner I get this over with, the less I'll have to see of him.

"I should have been inside with Mama, not outside playing. But there were so many people in the house. And a lot of them were talking loud and laughing and eating all that food like it was some kind of party or something. I just had to get the heck out of there. Daddy, Danny, Grandma, and Grandpa were about the only ones who even acted sad that Mama was gone. Plus Sister Grimes was there."

"And Sister Grimes made you uncomfortable."

"She accused me of killing Mama."

Frank lets out a big sigh and leans forward, resting his elbows on his knees. His usual Mr. Potato Head snap-on smile is different now. It looks almost . . . *real*.

"Mrs. Grimes said a thoughtless, horrible thing, and I'm sorry you overheard it, Riley. But she didn't cause your mama to get cancer and neither did you. Sometimes bad things happen to good people. Okay?"

I nod. I guess Frank's not all bad. But he should stick to talking to psycho kids and never go into law enforcement.

"So you went back inside the house," he says.

I nod again. "I wanted to see Mama one last time."

"And what did she look like to you, Riley?"

I think about this a minute. "She sort of looked like herself, but sort of not. She looked peaceful. I wanted to touch her to make sure she was really gone and not just sleeping."

"So what did you do?"

I stare at Frank a minute before answering, still feeling guilty about what I did.

"I pushed the sheet back from her hand and touched it." I know what Frank's going to ask next, so I go ahead and tell him. "Her skin was really cold. It didn't feel like real skin. Kind of hard and waxy. I didn't like the way it felt. But then I saw her wedding ring."

I pause to see if Frank will let me just skip ahead, but nope, he wants the whole enchilada.

"Mama used to let me play with her wedding ring. She'd let me put it on sometimes, just for fun. I thought it would be nice to have something of hers and I didn't think she would mind. The preacher said at the funeral that Mama wasn't in that body anymore, anyway. And nobody would ever know."

"So you remember taking the ring?"

I nod. "Most everyone was in the den. A few people were in the living room but they weren't paying me no mind. They were talking to Daddy and Danny. So I slipped the ring off her finger, put it in my pocket, and pulled the sheet back up over her hand. Nobody even saw me."

Frank nods and smiles at me like I just won a spelling bee or something. I probably could win a spelling bee. I know a lot of words, thanks to Mama.

"That's good, Riley," he says. "Very good. Then what happened?"

"I went back outside to hang out with Gary and Carl. A little later, the men from the funeral home rolled Mama's casket out the front door and put it into the big white limousine—"

Frank stops me with a raised unibrow.

"—hearse."

A *hearse* is a big white limousine taxi for dead people. Sometimes they can be black too.

As in, *I'll bet hearse drivers never get tipped by their passengers.*

Frank grins at me. I don't know if he's more proud of me for remembering everything the right way now or because he thinks he cured me.

"And finally, Riley," Frank says, "how about the Whispers?"

"What about them?" I say.

Frank leans back in his chair. "Can we agree that you have quite the imagination? And that's not a bad thing, mind you. But do you still think you heard them speaking to you?"

"It's just a story my mama told me," I say, shaking my head. Yeah, I thought the blue ghost fireflies were the Whispers, but I'll never believe I didn't hear them. Or someone. Maybe it was Mama calling to me. Maybe she wanted me to find her grave and remember everything so I could get better and so Daddy and Danny could heal too. All I know is I heard something. But Frank never has to know that. Nobody does.

"Sort of like the story you told yourself," Frank says. "One in which your mother was still alive and could possibly return home. It's called childhood traumatic grief. You and your mother were extremely close. You feel her loss very deeply."

I think about what he said. "Is that why I started wetting the bed, too?"

Frank nods. "That would make sense, yes."

"Am I cured now?" I ask, even though I haven't felt sick at all.

Franks smiles and shakes his head. "There was never anything to cure, Riley. You just had to find your way back to accepting reality instead of creating an alternate narrative. Do you understand what that means?"

I nod. And I do understand now. My head and my heart have been working overtime to protect me the last few months.

"Good." Frank glances up at the clock on the wall. "That's our time for today."

I can't get up off that Fritos-smelling couch fast enough. I'm halfway to the door when Frank calls out to me. I stop and look over my shoulder at him.

"We'll just meet one or two more times," he says. "Just to check in. But I think you're going to be just fine."

Instead of rolling my eyes like I want to, I just smile at him and get the heck out of there.

Daddy's the only person waiting in the lobby and he stands when I come out. He looks plumb worn-out. I'm afraid that's my fault. I guess he was real worried when Dylan told him I was out there in the woods by myself. He doesn't look mad, though. He's actually smiling at me a little. I walk over to him and he squats down in front of me just like Dylan Mathews, King of the Redneck Superheroes, did at Mama's grave.

He raises his eyebrows. "How did it go?"

"I told Frank everything," I say. "The *real* everything."

I didn't plan on crying, but it sneaks up on me and a couple of tears escape out of my eyeballs, maybe because I'm scared to death to do what I'm about to do. I slip my hand down into my front right pocket and pull out the Ziploc bag with Mama's wedding ring. Daddy stares at it with a blank look, his smile fading.

"I'm sorry, Daddy," I say. "I took it the day of the wake. I just wanted—"

He covers my hand and the bag with his and stops me with a serious look. I don't know if he's mad, or sad, or about to turn me in to the *real* police.

"I knew you took it," he says.

It takes a couple of seconds for my brain to catch up with my ears, and when it does, I just about fall over like I've been slain in the spirit.

Traces of his smile return. "I saw you take it."

I stare at him, not knowing how to respond. He knew I had the ring this whole time. "And you're not mad?"

His eyes soften. "I was at first. *Very* mad. But that was just my grief reacting. I realized pretty quick that your mama would want you to have it. And you've done such a good job keeping it safe, do you think you could keep doing that for me?"

I feel like the weight of the entire world has been lifted off my shoulders. I smile back at him and stuff the Ziploc bag back into my pocket so Daddy knows it will be safe.

"I'm sorry I made you all so sad by being a crazy person."

Daddy coughs out a laugh and hangs his head. "Don't call yourself crazy, son."

"What would you call it, then?"

When he looks up at me again, his eyes are soaking wet with tears. "Unique. Special. Exceptional."

He pulls me to him and hugs me so tight I can barely breathe. "I was so scared when I thought I'd lost you, too."

I slip my arms around him and rest my head on his shoulder, burying my face in his neck just like I did to Tucker at Mama's grave. Daddy smells better than Tucker.

We just stay there in Dr. Frank's poorly decorated lobby holding each other for like I don't know how long. Finally Daddy pulls back and looks at me.

"You know those words are all synonyms for each other," I say.

Daddy looks confused.

"*Unique. Special. Exceptional.* They all kind of mean the same thing."

"Oh yeah, right," he says with a big smile. A real live smile, like from old Daddy. "Do they make a word-of-the-day desk calendar for synonyms?"

We both giggle a little bit and he pokes me in the side.

"Maybe you can help me with my vocabulary," he says. He looks at me a minute without saying anything. Then he says, "I can't lose you like that again."

I don't want him to cry any more, so I give him my best snarky smile. "*Can't* never could and *If* never would."

That makes him laugh and he stands up, running his fingers through his dark wavy hair.

"I'm so sorry for not being more patient with you, son," he says, putting his hand on the top of my head, just like I used to do to Tucker. "I wasn't there for you and Danny like you needed." He pulls me in for a second bear hug, leans down, and whispers in my ear, "And you never have to hide anything from me. You're perfect just the way you are."

For a split second I panic and feel like all that pee I've been saving up the last few nights of dry sheets is about to shoot right out of me like one of those busted fire hydrants on *CID: Chicago*. Mama must have told him about Kenny from Kentucky. Of course she did. They told each other everything. Daddy knows about *my other condition*. And it doesn't matter. He still loves me.

Daddy guides me over to the door with a hand on my shoulders. "So what do you think for dinner? Fish sticks and Tater Tots, or your grandma's fried chicken?"

I look up at him and roll my eyes, but not in a disrespectful way. He knows the answer. Grandma's fried chicken is no joke. Everybody in Buckingham County knows that.

Daddy smiles. "Okay, fish sticks it is."

"Daddy," I whine.

He laughs. "I'm just joshin' you, Button."

I grin so hard my face feels like it's about to crack open. It's the first time Daddy has ever called me Button.

27

GOOD NIGHT, MY LOVE

I stand in the backyard that evening at twilight, staring out at the Pentecostal corn choir. The sun is setting, the honeysuckle breeze is rolling in, and the choir members shuffle their lanky, leafy selves around, waiting for my cue. Nature's symphony is tuning up all around us, getting ready for the big show.

Gazing out at the tree line of the woods in the distance, I can't help but smile. I don't expect to hear *the* Whispers anymore, but I'll always listen for whispers in the wind. If that's where Mama is, or if she's upstairs with Jesus and Tucker in heaven, I know she's watching me right now and smiling down on me. And Daddy, Danny, Grandma, Grandpa, even me—we'll all be okay. Mama spent her whole life taking care of people, no reason to think she'll stop now.

It's time for this evening's performance to begin. I'm the featured soloist, so I turn around and face the back of our house. The empty porch swing rocks back and forth in the breeze like it did the last time I sat there with Mama on a night just like this. Now I can remember it like it was yesterday.

"I want to talk to you about that day in the shed," Mama says.

I freeze. I stop breathing for a second, too. I didn't think Mama would ever want to talk about that day. I know I don't.

I look up at her nervously. "Can you forgive me?"

Her face sags and instant tears cloud her graying eyes.

"Sweetie," she says, shaking her head. "There's nothing to forgive. I was just surprised is all."

I breathe a little easier and break away from her gaze. "And you still love me?"

She sighs and relaxes her shoulders. "Button, do you know what unconditional *means?"*

I kind of do, but I like to hear her definitions, so I shake my head like I don't.

Mama squints her eyes into the setting sun. Her hair is gone but she doesn't try to hide her bald head. She calls it a badge of honor. I think she looks like a beauty queen with or without hair.

"It means there are no rules or boundaries, or expectations, no matter what." She looks back at me, smiling. "Make sense?"

I nod. "Use it in a sentence, Mama."

"That's an easy one." She slips her arm around me and pulls me close to her. "My love for you is unconditional, Button."

"No matter what?" I ask.

"No matter what." She smiles and nods once. Like a period. End of story.

That makes me warm from the inside out. Then she starts humming the song—the lullaby she used to sing to me every night after telling me the story of the Whispers.

The memory is like my intro, so I clear my throat, step forward, and sing the first verse as loud as I can so she can hear me wherever she might be.

> *Good night, my love, it's time to go to sleep*
> *And let all your worries float away*

My eyes itch and instantly blur with tears.

> *I will be here when you wake again*
> *To love and keep you through another day*

My voice cracks and my throat closes up. I take a deep breath, exhale, and keep going. I have to do this for Mama. I have to say goodbye.

> *And until then I'll hold you in my arms*
> *And rock you peacefully into dreams*
> *Think of me up with the stars*

A sob chokes me, stealing my voice away completely, and I'm not sure I can get through it after all. But then a forceful gust of wind presses against my face and swaddles me into a hug, just like she's here. I close my eyes and lean into it, breathing in the sweet honeysuckle fragrance of her memory. She's standing next to me now, like she used to when we directed the Pentecostal corn choir together. Her dark hair is long and wavy again, her cheeks rosy red. She looks as young and beautiful as she did the day of the Christmas parade all those years ago. Her presence gives me the strength to find my voice again.

As you drift away to other lands
All of the things that you mean to me, I hope you understand

Nature's symphony fades in, right on cue. Mama and I turn to face our corn choir members together. We raise our hands and bring them in on the downbeat for the next verse. The wind makes the choir all sway together in perfect time as they sing. They sound amazing—especially my tenors and basses.

Good night, my love, it's time to sail away
On magic oceans to a moonlit sea
And if the waves rage all around
You'll always wake up safe with me

I cue Mama to take the solo on the last verse and nature's symphony swells to accompany her. I just stand there listening to her voice fill the twilight sky, like a thousand whispers in the wind.

And now, my love, it's time to say goodbye
Though I promise you are not alone
Through wind and through rain and stormy nights
My voice will always guide you home

As the warm honeysuckle breeze slowly fades away, it brushes my cheek and tickles my nose one last time.

Good night, Button.

I guess I can't be sure it's Mama's voice I hear. My head and my heart could be making up stories again. But why not hope?

So I whisper back, just in case. "Good night, Mama."

AUTHOR'S NOTE

First, a confession. Blue ghost fireflies (*Phausis reticulate*) would not be found in a forest in South Carolina as they are in this story. It's a rare species that appears for two to four weeks only in the Blue Ridge and Great Smoky Mountains. I took some liberties with those facts because after my first experience with these unique creatures, I just knew they were the key to telling Riley's story. Also, I felt that their unlikely appearance in the setting of this book added to the sense of magic and wonder. Thank you for allowing me the latitude to make that choice.

Second, the inspiration. My mother died of cancer at the age of twenty-six. I was five years old. At the time, I didn't really understand what was going on, and the adults around me were so consumed by their own grief that they couldn't even talk about my mother, much less explain to me what happened to her. It wasn't until I was in my forties that I had the courage to even ask my father what type of cancer she had. After Mama died, he shut down emotionally, and my brother and I were left to navigate life without her on our own. Pictures of her were taken down because it was too hard for the adults to see them. Family photo albums disappeared. Her clothes and belongings were given away. When my father remarried a few years later, my brother and I were forced to call this strange woman in our house *Mama*. It was as if my mother never existed. I was a mama's boy without a mama—without a compass. And the sudden isolation from her and her memory was devastating.

My childhood grief over the loss of my mother didn't manifest itself as elaborately as Riley's, but I did seek refuge in my imagination. For example, in the absence of hearing stories and family members sharing memories about her as the years passed, I created my own. One such memory was of my beauty pageant queen mother riding on the back of an open convertible in the Christmas parade as the newly crowned "Mrs. Georgetown." There was a sign on the side of the car with Mama's name printed on it. She wore a white hat and white gloves, and had a red corsage pinned to her dress. She was beautiful and looked like South Carolina's own Jackie Kennedy. For years I remembered vividly standing on the sidewalk as she waved to me from the back of that convertible. I beamed with pride at my mama, Mrs. Georgetown, South Carolina, and waved back like crazy. It was a memory that gave me great comfort for a long time.

Some years later, an old family photo of that day resurfaced. I can't remember from where or from whom, but I was an adult when it fell into my possession. When I saw it, I realized that my memory of that day was completely self-manufactured. It was the faded color picture I remembered, not the moment itself. Because scribbled in the bottom border in my dad's handwriting was *Miss Georgetown Contestant* and a date, three years before I was born. In truth, Mama was only a contestant in the Miss Georgetown Pageant (not the *Mrs.* Georgetown Pageant) and I wasn't there at all. I'm not even sure it was a Christmas parade.

Childhood traumatic grief may occur with the unexpected loss or even the anticipated death of a parent or loved one. One of the effects on the child can be the creation of an alternative narrative, possibly one in which there is hope of the deceased loved one returning, as in *The Whispers*. To put it into Riley's own simple words, your head and your heart tell you a different story in order to protect you. And like Riley, I don't think my head and my heart meant any harm by creating memories out of faded photographs. They were just looking out for me. So, I forgive them.

For more information on childhood traumatic grief, contact the National Child Traumatic Stress Network at nctsn.org.

Turn the page for a sneak peek of
Greg Howard's latest book

1

THE OFFICE

I sit behind the huge oak desk in my office at the world headquarters of Anything, Incorporated, organizing my homework like I do every Sunday afternoon. I spend a lot of weekends in the office. If I didn't, I'd never get anything done. I think CEOs of big-time companies like mine shouldn't be required to attend middle school. It seriously gets in the way of doing important business stuff.

I've created an Excel spreadsheet on my laptop and sorted my assignments into three columns:

```
Teacher Will Check
Teacher Won't Check
Teacher Will Collect but Won't Check
```

Normally I'd have my assistant handle this kind of thing, but she quit last week. It's okay, though, because she was a climber. More interested in having a fancy title than doing a good job for the company. She started as an intern about a month ago, recommended by one of our board members. She was terrible even back then. I could never find a stapler when I needed one, and my printer was always out of paper. I thought if I gave her a real title and some responsibility by promoting her to assistant to the president, she'd step up her game. But she didn't. All she wanted to do was criticize me. Her boss! That's not how it works in the corporate world.

I open my "Brilliant Business Tips" Excel spreadsheet, scroll down to the next empty cell, and type:

Michael Pruitt Business Tip #347: There's only one way to the top. Keep your head down, apply yourself, and do your time.

It sure would be nice to have someone handle all this busywork now that my assistant bailed on me. I'd much rather be spending my time doing real boss stuff, like planning my next exciting business venture. Retail wasn't the right fit for me. Neither was professional sports instruction. But I have a million other ideas. Those are just two recent ones that didn't work out.

Pap Pruitt always says, *If at first you don't succeed, try, try again.*

I've had my share of failures, but I never give up. I know I'll have a successful business empire one day just like my hero, Pap Pruitt. Technically Pap is my grandfather. He taught me everything I know about business.

My desk first belonged to Pap when he started his real

estate business at seventeen years old. When Pap moved into the nursing home, Dad didn't need it for his landscaping business, so he lets me use it. It's a real boss-looking desk and I always feel real important sitting at it. I also feel close to Pap when I'm at my desk. He's been in the nursing home for a while now, and I don't get to see him as much. Plus he's sick a lot, so Dad doesn't always let me go with him to visit Pap. He didn't let me go today, which I guess is why Pap's been on my mind.

Pap was a super-crazy-successful entrepreneur when he was younger. He started his own general store, a dry cleaning business, two fast-food franchises, a hotel called the Old Pruitt Place, a pet-grooming business, a landscaping business, *three* auto-matic car washes, a boiled-peanut roadside stand, and a whole lot more. I asked him once how he became so successful. I remember the sparkle in his eye when he grinned a little and said, *All it takes is a dream and a prayer.*

I've got lots of dreams. And even though I'm not the best at prayers, the Almighty is pretty used to hearing from me when it comes to a new business idea. Pap started his business empire in his garage with only a hundred dollars, a dream, and a prayer. Pap's blind now because of the diabetes, but he's still a wicked-cool guy. I really want to make him proud, but he didn't have to build his business empire *and* go to middle school at the same time. I guess Pap was a late bloomer.

It's a little embarrassing, having to do homework at your real job. I'll bet Malcolm Forbes never had to do that and he was, like, one of the most successful business guys ever. Luckily my office is pretty private, but that doesn't always keep the riffraff out. Sometimes it can get so noisy in here, especially when the dryer's on its last cycle like it is now. It sounds like a space shuttle getting ready to launch. And there must be a shoe in there, because something bangs against the side every few seconds, distracting me from my work. I lean back in my executive, fake-leather desk chair and stare at Dad's tools hanging on the wall, waiting for the banging to stop.

The annoyingly long honk of the buzzer sounds and the pounding inside the machine finally fades away. I hit the Talk button on the intercom on my desk.

"Mom," I say, pretty loud so she can hear me from anywhere inside the house. And because I'm annoyed that there's a washer and dryer in my office.

No response.

I hit the button again. "Mom!"

A few seconds later, her voice crackles through the intercom speaker. "Yes, Mikey, what is it?"

I sigh and press the Talk button. "Mom, I asked you not to call me that when I'm at work."

"Oh, sorry, honey. *Michael*, what is it? Is the dryer done?"

We've talked about *honey*, too, but I'm too busy to get into that right now.

"Yes, ma'am," I say.

"Okay," she says. "I'll be right there."

Dad found the old-timey intercom system at a garage sale

and hooked it up for me. It's lime green and nearly the size of a shoe box, but at least it works. Dad thought it'd be a perfect addition to my office and an easy way for Mom to call me in for dinner. Dad gets it.

Mom comes through the carport door—*without knocking*—carrying a laundry basket.

"Mom, the sign's out," I say. "You're supposed to knock when the sign's out."

"It's getting late, honey. I thought you'd be closing up shop by now."

She's wearing light blue mom shorts and one of Dad's old white button-down shirts.

"I'm rebranding," I say. "It takes a lot of thinking time."

Wait a minute. That would be a cool business idea. I could be an expert at helping businesses rebrand. Like I could go down to the Burger King on Palmetto Street and pitch them the idea of updating their brand to make it more modern and hip. The first thing they need to do is change their name to something more welcoming of all people instead of just men. Something like Burger Person or Burger Human Being would be a good choice. I open up my spiral-bound *Amazing Business Ideas* notebook and write that new business idea down before I forget.

Anything Modern and Hip Rebranding
A division of Anything, Inc.
Michael Pruitt—President, Founder, CEO, and Brand Expert

"So how come the putt-putt lessons didn't work out?"

"*Croquet* lessons, Mom," I say. "Not putt-putt."

"Oh, right," she says. "We used to play croquet all the time when I was a kid."

"I know," I say.

Grandma Sharon gave me their old set of clubs and balls and taught me how to play last summer. None of the kids in the neighborhood had ever heard of croquet, which was perfect because it made me the local expert. I might have added a few new rules to the game to make it more interesting, but my students never knew the difference.

Mom rests the basket of towels on her hip. A shoe sits on top. I wonder why she only washed one. It's a perplexing mystery.

I write down another incredible idea in my *Amazing Business Ideas* notebook:

Anything Perplexing Mystery-Solving Detective Agency
A division of Anything, Inc.
Michael Pruitt—President, Founder, CEO, and Head Snoop

I put a star beside that one because that's a super-crazy-good idea.

"Well, how many kids signed up for croquet lessons?" Mom asks.

Before I can answer, my little sister, Lyla, appears in the doorway cradling her fat gray cat in her arms. The cat's name is Pooty. Lyla named him that because he farts a lot. I hate that cat.

"He had four students show up for the first lesson," she says with all the innocence of a possessed doll in a horror movie. "They each paid him a dollar, if you can believe that. But no one showed up for the second lesson. He made four dollars, but he gave them each a whole bottle of water, so he probably lost money."

"I haven't run the final numbers yet," I say, looking back at my spreadsheet, trying to ignore Lyla and her gassy cat.

"And kids around here don't know what croquet is anyway," she adds like she's some kind of marketing expert. She's nine.

"That was the beauty of it," I snap back. "Nobody knew if I was teaching it wrong or not."

"It was a dumb idea, if you ask me," she says.

"You were a dumb idea," I mumble under my breath.

"Mikey! That's enough," Mom says.

"She started it," I say in a pouty voice that makes me sound like a little kid.

Mom shifts the laundry basket to her other hip. "She's only nine. Be a better example."

That's Mom's excuse for everything Lyla does. *She's only seven. She's only eight. She's only nine.* You see where this is heading, right? It's never going to end.

"Sorry," I say, even though secretly I'm not.

Lyla smiles at me like she won or something.

There are no trophies for being possessed by the devil, Lyla!

"I'll give a full report on the Sports Instruction division of the company at the next board meeting," I say.

She kisses me on top of the head. "Sounds good, honey."

I sigh. I don't think she's ever going to get the *honey* thing. And don't even get me started on the kiss.

Mom leaves, but Lyla still stands in the doorway. Both she and Pooty glare at me. The cat hates me as much as I hate him. He always stares at me like he's planning to murder me. That's why I lock my bedroom door every night before I go to bed. You just never know with cats.

"So what's your next big idea, Mikey?" Lyla says, stroking Pooty's head like an old movie villain who's trying to take over the world. I wouldn't put it past her, even though *she's only nine*.

"It's Michael when I'm in the office," I say. "You know that."

She looks around the cramped, unfinished space with tools hanging on the walls like they're standing guard. "You mean our carport-storage-and-laundry room?"

I turn my back to her, attacking the keys of my laptop like I'm typing a really important email. "You didn't mind it when you worked here."

I hear the door close behind me.

Thank God. She left.

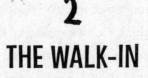

2
THE WALK-IN

"My talent was being wasted."

Or maybe not.

Lyla sits in the metal folding chair beside my desk; it used to be her work area. I asked for a cubicle wall to put between us for privacy, but the board denied the request. They said it wasn't in the budget.

"You were my assistant, but you wanted me to make you junior vice president of the company." I shake my head at her. "Not going to happen. You're too young and you don't have enough business experience."

She swings her legs. "Your loss."

Pooty settles into a ball on her lap, staring at me like he's going to eat me. I shake my head again and look back at the spreadsheet. My sister is three years younger than me, but she acts like we're the same age. Or like she's my *older* sister. She's always been weird that way. Mom calls her *precocious*. I call her *pain in the butt*.

A three-rap knock sounds at the door.

"Come in, Dad," I call. Dad never forgets to knock when the sign is out.

He hurries over to his wall of tools. "Sorry to bother you, Michael. Just need to grab the spatula for the grill. I'm making burgers."

Forbes, my cocker spaniel, follows Dad through the door, but Pooty hisses at Forbes and he retreats with a whine. Pooty's a bully and Forbes is his favorite target. Poor Forbes. Pooty would fit right in with Tommy Jenrette and his jerk friends at school.

Lyla looks up at Dad and plasters on the big baby smile she's way too old to still be using. "Dad, did you know that Mikey's latest business idea was a humongous flop?"

Dad looks over at me. "Oh no. Is that right, Michael?"

I look away, mumbling back: "You'll get a full report at the next board meeting."

"Oh, okay, then," he says, and I can hear the support in his voice.

Like I said, Dad gets it. He built A to Z Landscaping from nothing to one of the busiest in southeastern North Charleston, in spite of the lame name. *Time to rebrand, Dad!* He even advertises in the *PennySaver* and the online Yellow Pages. Pap Pruitt taught him well.

"How was Pap today?" I ask, my voice tightening around the words.

Dad's face sags. Not a good sign.

"Not great," he says, fake-smiling. "But he's hanging in

there. He asked about you. Maybe he'll be well enough for you to visit him next Sunday."

A lump swells in my throat and I swallow it back. I just nod and fake-smile back at him.

"I want to go see Pap, too, Daddy," Lyla whines.

Dad musses her hair. "Like I said, honey. We'll see."

After the shadow of sadness fades from Dad's face, he grabs the big metal spatula off the wall over my desk. "Dinner in twenty, okay?"

"Okay, Daddy." Lyla says, baby-smile wattage at one hundred.

"And don't worry, son," he says. "I bet your next idea will be the one. Pap is so proud of you. I am, too."

I don't say anything because I'm afraid my voice will fail me. I know Pap and Dad are already proud of me. But we all know that Pap won't be around too much longer. I just want him to see my first big success.

Pooty yawns very disrespectfully as Dad closes the door behind him. I fake-type some more, hoping Lyla will get the hint and go, too. My eyes are itching and no little sister wants to see her big brother cry. Not even Lyla. But she doesn't get the hint. She just sits there swinging her legs and stroking Pooty's back.

"Don't you have homework?"

"Already finished," she says. "What are you working on?"

"None of your business," I say. "You didn't want to work here anymore, remember?"

She cocks her head. "I never said I didn't want to work here. I just wanted a better job than being your dumb assistant."

Before I can respond, there's another knock on the door. Maybe Mom remembered this time.

"Come in," I call out. I can't get anything done today with all these interruptions. I bet Pap Pruitt never had to put up with this.

The door creaks open behind me, but Lyla doesn't say anything, so I spin around in my chair. Standing in the doorway is a kid I kind of recognize from school, but I don't remember his name. I think he's in the eighth grade and I don't hang out with any eighth graders. I only recognize him at all because he's the *wrong* kind of popular at North Charleston Middle. And I've got enough problems at school without hanging out with kids who are the wrong kind of popular.

Lyla and I just stare at him, which I know is super-crazy rude and unprofessional but I can't help it. He's wearing sandals, neatly pressed jeans, and a white tank top with You Better Werk! printed on the front. He's taller than me and thick all over. Especially in the stomach area. After an awkward silence, the boy finally speaks up.

"Is this Anything, Incorporated?" he says, glancing around the room with stank face, like my office is the inside of a garbage dumpster. But I can't even be mad at him for that because—*OMG!*—he knows the name of my company. How wicked cool is that?

He glances over at the washer and dryer and then back to me. "I mean the sign on the door says so, but—"

"Yes!" I say a little too excitedly.

I snap out of my surprise at having someone who was actually looking for my office who's not a member of my family and who didn't think this was a laundromat or a hardware store or anything. I've never had a walk-in before.

I stand, extending my hand to him and clearing my throat. "I'm Michael Pruitt, president, founder, and chief executive officer of Anything, Inc."

The boy steps inside from our carport, closing the door behind him. He takes my hand and shakes it. His grip is loose and kind of clammy but he has a bright smile and sparkly eyes framed with—*is that glitter?*

"Yeah, I know," he says, letting go of my hand, still looking around my office, but without the stank face now. "We go to the same school."

"Mikey doesn't have any friends at school," Lyla says, looking down at Pooty, scratching his head. "They all think he's a weirdo loser and that all his business ideas are lame because none of them have ever worked."

And OMG!

I glare at her, my face heating from the inside out. Why did I ever trust her with sensitive company secrets? The boy looks like he doesn't know how to respond to that. Who would?

I clear my throat, plastering on my fake smile again. "Of

course I have friends, Lyla. You remember Trey and Dinesh. We've been friends since first grade."

Lyla smirks and shakes her head. "Nope. Never heard of them."

I grit my teeth through the fake smile. "Don't you have somewhere to be, Lyla? Somewhere that's not here. Like your room? Or China?"

The boy coughs into his elbow. Pooty poots. I wave the air around with my hand like I'm trying to swat a fly so my walk-in customer doesn't smell it.

"I bought a candy bar at your general store one time," he says, like he didn't notice Murder Kitty's gas attack. "I thought that store was a pretty cool idea. It was in a good location and had plenty of candy bars and other snacks that kids like. I got the chocolate one with peanut butter and nuts."

Pride curls my whole face into a grin. "That was one of my bestsellers. Could hardly keep them in stock."

"You sold three," Lyla pipes up matter-of-factly. "I was in charge of inventory, remember?" She looks over at the boy and sighs, like being a pain in the butt is so exhausting for her. "The Anything General Store got blown away by a baby tornado three days after the grand opening."

I swear to God.

The boy gives me a sympathetic look. "Oh. Sorry. I wondered why it was gone so fast. I came back the next week for another candy bar."

My face flushes hot again. "My dad built the store out of

15

big sheets of cardboard, so, you know—lesson learned."

Dad did a great job on the store. He built it in the front yard close to the foot traffic of the sidewalk. He said that's called *location, location, location*. The store had a wooden frame of two-by-fours, a flip-up sales counter/window, and a real door in back. Well, a real cardboard door. But the store was no match for a baby tornado. Lost all my inventory, too. Our next-door neighbor, Mrs. Brown, thought her bunny rabbit, Hedwig, started pooping magic pellets. I didn't have the heart to tell her they were just Skittles.

The boy nods and smiles at me like he understands. I think it's kind of nice of him.

I point at Lyla, trying to be professional. "This is my *former* associate, Lyla Pruitt, and her gassy and very unfriendly cat, Pooty. They were just leaving."

"Hey," the boy says, waving at Lyla with a big, wide smile.

She stands, but doesn't say anything. She doesn't even smile back. Instead, she hefts Pooty up to her chest, giving my walk-in that creepy-kid stare of hers as she takes her sweet time leaving. It's extremely unprofessional.

Michael Pruitt Business Tip #348: Human-demon dolls make terrible receptionists.

I learned that one the hard way.

ACKNOWLEDGMENTS

My amazing editor, Stacey Barney—where do I begin? Your passion for this book was evident during our very first phone conversation and then by how you simply would NOT take no for an answer until you got the book. (I mean, like, we considered getting a restraining order.) You weren't going down without a fight and without convincing me that Putnam was the perfect (and only) home for *The Whispers*. Of course, you were right. Working with you and the Putnam team has been a dream from the beginning to the end of the process. I could not be happier to be part of the Putnam/PRH family and look forward to crafting many more stories with you in the years to come. Most of all, this book would have been woefully incomplete without your superb (sometimes annoyingly so) editorial direction. And thank you for making me feel special—like a real live author person.

My own personal boho-Barbie superhero, Bri Johnson (aka B-Jo, aka the best agent in the history of agents!)—you have worked your butt off for me since day one and I appreciate it SO much. My life has changed and it all started with you taking a chance on me. *The Whispers* truly would not be the book it is if not for you. Your initial editorial insights pushed me to dig deeper and take this thing to a *whole nother level*. You believed in this book and encouraged me to run with it before anyone else caught the vision. Thanks for holding my hand through the big scary publishing auction storm and navigating this ship safely to shore. (And a big shout-out to our Lindas!)

Cecilia de la Campa and the subrights team at Writers House—thank you for getting Riley's story told around the world and in so many different languages. Hopefully I will finally learn Spanish by reading my own book. How meta would that be?! (*mind blown*)

Vivienne To—I won the lottery with this cover and your gorgeous, on-point illustration is a huge part of the reason why. I knew you were good, but dang! I realize now how lucky we were to get you on this project, because I don't think anyone else could have nailed it like you did. Thank you for sharing your amazing talent with me and the world.

Lindsey Andrews—thanks for your guidance with the cover design, pulling all the perfect elements (and people) together and allowing my input throughout the process. I can't begin to tell you how much I love it!

Courtney Gilfillian at Putnam and Allie Levick at Writers House—you guys keep all of us on track and pick up the many balls that I drop. Thank you and count me as a lifelong fan!

Emma Jones at Puffin/Random House UK—thank you for your passion for *The Whispers* from the beginning. Whether you realize it or not, the enthusiastic support of the UK team helped seal the deal!

Mary Pender at UTA—thank you so much for believing in this book and its message WAY early and for taking such care with its journey from page to screen. You are a game-changer.

Thank you, thank you, thank you, Luke McMaster and Arun Chaturvedi, for breathing musical life into my "Good Night, My Love" lyrics. It's just so beautiful and perfect, I could pee myself.

To all the librarians, booksellers, teachers, bloggers, and reviewers who have recommended *The Whispers*, please know how much I appreciate it and never doubt that you are changing lives every day. *"That is part of the beauty of all literature. You discover that your longings are universal longings, that you're not lonely and isolated from anyone. You belong."*—F. Scott Fitzgerald

Steve—you were my loudest cheerleader while writing this book. You got excited about every tiny bit of book news I shared with you. You shielded me from the happiness vampires. You took all my story questions seriously and didn't sugarcoat your opinions. And you reminded me to say *when* instead of *if* regarding all the exciting possibilities of this journey. I am forever grateful for your friendship.

GREG HOWARD was born and raised in the South Carolina Lowcountry, where his love of words and stories blossomed at a young age. Originally set on becoming a songwriter, Greg followed that dream to the bright lights of Nashville, Tennessee, and spent years producing the music of others before eventually returning to his childhood passion of writing stories. Greg writes young-adult and middle-grade novels focusing on LGBTQ characters and issues. He has an unhealthy obsession with Reese's Peanut Butter Cups and currently resides in Nashville with his three rescued fur babies—Molly, Toby, and Riley.

Connect with Greg at greghowardbooks.com
or on Facebook, Instagram, and Twitter:
@greghowardbooks